FROM THE AUTH

My Jacks — I a
inspired by my wonderful, crazy family
and the people I love. When you read these
books, I am inviting you inside my home
to meet fantastic characters — the nanna
who is obsessed with buying bargains, the
step-dad who is the best dish washer in the
whole world, the sister who loves dogs, the mum (me) who
does the best star jumps possible, and of course Jack.

We live in Sydney and we went on a great holiday up
north, to the Gold Coast. There were so many adventures on
the way as well as when we got there — everything from
dolphins to cane toads to the Tower of Terror. I want to thank
Dreamworld and their amazing Bengal tigers and Sea World
with their awesome polar bears for making it an even better
time. I write about the trip north in *SuperJack* and about
being a family, with all the funny, sad and happy parts.

I love being an author. I used to be a teacher, which I loved
too. I loved helping recreate The Hughenden, which is a
beautiful heritage hotel in Sydney, associated with Australia's
first philosopher. I absolutely love my kids — except when
they are making a huge mess inside the house.

I wrote *SuperJack* for my family, for the people I care about
and for you.

'*I Am Jack* and *SuperJack* celebrate kids, just as
Life Education Australia does.'

LIFE EDUCATION AUSTRALIA

Visit Susanne Gervay's website at:
www.sgervay.com

Other books by Susanne Gervay

I am Jack
Always Jack
Being Jack
Butterflies
The Cave
Jamie's a Hero
Next Stop the Moon
Shadows of Olive Trees
That's Why I Wrote This Song
Daisy Sunshine

Picture books
Ships in the Field
Gracie and Josh
Elephants Have Wings

Susanne Gervay

Illustrated by Cathy Wilcox

SUPER Jack

Angus&Robertson
An imprint of HarperCollins*Children's*Books

Angus&Robertson
An imprint of HarperCollins*Children'sBooks*, Australia

First published in 2003
by HarperCollins*Publishers* Australia Pty Limited
ABN 36 009 913 517
harpercollins.com.au

HarperCollins*Publishers*
Level 13, 201 Elizabeth Street, Sydney NSW 2000, Australia
Unit D, 63 Apollo Drive, Rosedale, Auckland 0632, New Zealand
A 53, Sector 57, Noida, UP, India
1 London Bridge Street, London SE1 9GF, United Kingdom
2 Bloor Street East, 20th floor, Toronto, Ontario M4W 1A8, Canada
195 Broadway NY, NY 10007, United States of America

National Library of Australia Cataloguing-in-publication data:

Gervay, Susanne.
  SuperJack.
  Children aged 8–12.
  ISBN 0 207 19918 3.
  1. Family life – Juvenile fiction. 2. Stepfamilies – Juvenile fiction.
  I. Wilcox, Cathy, 1963– . II. Title.
A823.3

Cover and internal illustrations by Cathy Wilcox
Cover and internal design by Gayna Murphy, HarperCollins Design Studio
Typeset by HarperCollins in 13/15 Berkely Book
Printed and bound in Australia by Griffin Press
The papers used by HarperCollins in the manufacture of this book are a natural,
recyclable product made from wood grown in sustainable plantation forests. The
fibre source and manufacturing processes meet recognised international
environmental standards, and carry certification.

To Nanna, Veronika Gervay,
who will never get old in our hearts.

Chapter 1

Fungus

Grunt, groan. 'It's coming.' Mum's face is radish-red. Her blonde hair is exploding into a fuzz ball. 'Stuck, stuck,' she yelps, then she starts rocking from side to side. Mum's daisy skirt swirls around her. Finally she sputters. 'It's nearly here.'

My sister Samantha crouches in front of Mum. 'Do you need help?'

'No, thank you, darling.' Mum shakes her head. She hasn't done this for a long time. Mum puffs and huffs, then puts her hands under her skirt. 'Wow . . . one . . . no . . .' laughing, 'I think there are two.'

Samantha inspects excitedly. 'Oh, they're perfect.' Mum smiles as Samantha dances around the coffee table, bumping into the side of it. She knocks down some of the photo frames on it.

I shout at her, 'Hey, don't wreck the table.' I made that coffee table for Mum. Even though it has one wobbly leg, it is an excellent table. Everyone says that, even Nanna. Samantha is really irritating. She is jumping up and down like a milkshake shaker. I can see the froth coming out of her head. No, no, it's only sherbet. Dizzy and fizzy. Ha, ha.

I stand up the photographs. 'Mum ONLY laid eggs, Samantha. Perfect? As if.' My sister is an exaggerator.

'They ARE perfect. And anyway, no one else's Mum can lay eggs.'

I think about that one. It is true. I don't know of one other mother who can do that. For a long time, I didn't know that it was just a game. I am twelve now, and too old to believe that Mum can lay eggs. Still, I pretend to believe. It makes Mum and Samantha happy.

Mum is giggling. 'I haven't done that for a while.' She flounces into the kitchen with Samantha running behind her. 'How do you want them? Scrambled or sunny side up?'

Samantha hates the drippy, gooey yolk, so she always asks for scrambled. Mum knows that.

'Sunny side up for me,' I call out.

It's the best breakfast today. This Saturday, Rob, our sort-of-step-dad, is working at the spare car parts warehouse. So it is Mum, Samantha and me. Just the three of us. I think that is why Mum laid eggs this morning. She hasn't done it for ages. Mum is usually too busy with her new job as a library assistant. This morning she actually slept in. She hardly ever does that.

'So how is your school assignment going, Samantha?'

Oh no, that is so boring. I give Mum a doggy woof. She laughs, then I start to explain all about my A-plus assignment on mouth-to-mouth resuscitation. The first aid course is the only good thing we've done at school this year.

'You can tell me all about your first aid course after Samantha.'

After? What's wrong with Mum? Samantha sticks her tongue out at me. I just know she will go on and on about her dog project. She is insane about dogs. Samantha even sleeps with Floppy, who is a huge, brown and white, stuffed, FLAT dog. How many FLAT dogs do you know? NONE. I've told her that lots of times. 'Floppy is a stupid FLAT dog. Flat tail, flat body, flat head. Dumb, dumb, dumb.' When I called Floppy 'dumb' last week, Samantha threw her lunch box at me. Since her lunch box had a left-over rotten banana in it, it was a disgusting thing to do. But I kept the banana. I am using it in my new fungus experiment. It has white mould growing up one side and green slime at the top. I think that's where Samantha took a bite.

Samantha has posters of dogs all over her walls. She really wants a puppy, but no one is allowed to have dogs in our block of units. She loves Dalmatians and has made her own spotty dog drawing. Actually, Samantha is a very good drawer. She has a specially signed Selby the Talking Dog poster, signed by Selby with an original paw print. She emails Selby the Talking Dog on a regular basis. Selby is her best friend. Can you believe that?

My best friend is Anna, who is twelve like me. She lives next door, above her parents' fruitology market. I know Mum likes Anna, because Mum laid an egg for her. She has never done that in front of any of my other friends, or even Rob or Nanna. Mum says laying an egg is very private.

Samantha's brown eyes flash as she describes every minute detail of her dog project to Mum. Paw prints, bones, dog tails. She has actually stuck dog tails (not real ones) along the border. There is a spotty cotton-bud tail for a Dalmatian, a stubby pencil for a fox terrier, a black wool tail for the killer guard dog. Then I see it. Fuzz tail. Ha, ha. Fuzz tail. It is soft and blonde and fluffy. My brain gets into gear. This is a tactical opportunity to divert Mum's attention away from Samantha's project.

'Hey Mum, your hair is stuck next to the fox terrier.'

'What?' Mum rubs her fuzzy blonde hair, checking for snags. Parts of her hair are always fluffed into curly knots.

I pretend to be serious and stare at Samantha's dog project. 'Sorry. Mistake. I thought that was your head, Mum.' Swallowing a laugh, I point to the poodle's tail glued into the corner of Samantha's project.

Mum is laughing. 'At least my hair isn't spiky like yours, Jack.' She pushes Samantha's project to the side of the table. 'I'll look at the rest of your work later,' she tells her. Samantha starts to complain, but stops when Mum says, 'Nanna will be here after lunch. She'll love looking at it with all of us.'

That is true. Nanna loves anything we do.

Mum flattens her exploding hair. Samantha squeezes Mum's hand.

'I have a few things to talk to you about.' Mum gives a crooked smile, so it can't be too serious. 'Firstly, about Nanna.'

I flip the poodle tail into a twist. Samantha tries to hit my hand. 'Missed.' Ha, ha.

'Don't, Jack.' Mum's voice is soft. 'Nanna needs more help.' She looks at Samantha, then me.

'I'll help her,' Samantha pipes in. Honestly, she is such a crawler. I'll help Nanna too, but I don't say it. Mum just knows that I will. Mum hugs Samantha.

'It's school holidays next week.' Yes, yes, excellent! 'I've been thinking about a trip away. It'll give us all time to work things out with Nanna and our family.' Nanna? Family? What is Mum talking about? Holidays. We always go to Port Macquarie and stay at Mum's friend's holiday house. Surf and ice cream. I love it there. 'It's going to be our first family holiday with everyone.' Mum hesitates. 'Rob is coming. And there's . . .'

Samantha doesn't let Mum finish. 'I love Rob.'

That is so soppy. Nearly vomit-producing. I stick my finger in my mouth and pretend to throw up. Rob, Rob, Rob. He moved in a few months ago FULL-TIME. Mum asked us if it was okay. But there was no choice. I had to say 'yes' even though there is NO room in our unit. Rob hardly fits into Mum's bedroom, so he had to put a lot of his stuff in the garage. It's lucky we have a garage. Straightaway Rob put a photo of his son Leo on my wobbly coffee table. I don't know why Rob sticks Leo in our faces all the time now. Before he moved in full-time he didn't. It's annoying.

'Mum, can I take Floppy on holidays?'

What is Samantha going on about? Floppy? She doesn't understand anything. This is about Rob, not a dumb flat stuffed dog. Samantha doesn't realise the BIG problem of Rob in Mum's bed all the time. She doesn't mind right now, but she will. There won't be any night when she can get into Mum's bed. Mum used to leave her door open on non-Rob days, so that Samantha and I could come in any time, especially when we needed something important. Now Samantha has to knock on Mum's door and Mum says 'come in', but I've never heard Rob say that.

I don't knock on Mum's door any more. Well, I never really did before. I'd just run into her room. Sometimes I would hit the door as I crashed past it. Mum never minded, even when she was asleep. Now, I have to make a loud stamping sound and when Mum hears me coming, she calls out, 'Is that you, Jack?'

Mum says Rob is our step-dad, but they don't wear wedding rings. Rob was married once before. That's where Leo comes from. Rob never used to talk about Leo. Maybe because Leo doesn't live in Sydney. Hey, I just remembered. Leo lives in Port Macquarie.

Samantha is STILL hugging Floppy. 'Wish I had a puppy.' She looks at Mum with big doggy eyes.

I think Samantha loves Rob because he pretends to be a dog. Before she goes to bed, he woofs at her door and scrambles around her room on his hands and knees. He does look like a dog when he's wagging his bum and sticking out his tongue. Rob nuzzles Samantha's arms and she rubs his short spiky hair. (Rob and I have the same haircut.) 'Woof, woof.' He tickles her. Mum laughs in the doorway. I pretend to be a dog too, but Rob isn't interested. He doesn't want me there and neither does Samantha. Rob is the dog and they both ignore me.

'You'll love where we're going.'

I look suspiciously at Mum. 'Is it Port Macquarie?'

'We're staying there overnight, on the way up. Rob wants to see Leo.' Mum crinkles her daisy skirt in her hands. 'We all do.'

A funny feeling flushes through me. I am not sure about this Leo. I don't even know him. Why is Rob changing everything?

'We're going somewhere else these holidays.'

'Where, where, where?' Samantha squeaks. She always squeaks when she is excited.

Mum makes us guess. Samantha guesses everywhere from the Snowy Mountains to the desert to the Barrier Reef. 'No. No. No.' Mum smiles, shaking her head.

Samantha isn't chubby, but her cheeks are. They are going red, which means she is thinking, really thinking.

I can't take it. 'Tell us, Mum. Just tell us.'

'I'll give you hints.' Mum enjoys torturing us with long-drawn-out clues. 'A marine biologist would like staying there.' 'It's warm.' 'You'll need swimming costumes.' 'There's fishing there.' 'Surfing.'

'A beach,' Samantha and I call out together.

Mum laughs. 'You're right, but not just any beach.' She pauses for dramatic tension. 'We're going to the Gold Coast!'

Samantha jumps around like a cocker spaniel, all drippy and waggy. Wow, theme parks, water slides, surfing. This is the best, best, best. Mum's face glows like a sunflower. What a great breakfast. We ask Mum lots and lots of questions until she is laughing. Then I have a great thought. My fungus will grow really well in hot weather.

'Mum, can I take my fungus?'

'No!' Samantha and Mum shout together.

Chapter 2

Jack's Spitting Toast

I can't wait to tell Anna about our holidays. Anna. Suddenly, I get this idea. Anna on holidays with us. Maybe Mum will let her come to the Gold Coast. It would be fantastic. I stuff my last piece of toast into my mouth and blurt out, 'Hey, Mum.' There is a splattering explosion as bits of toast catapult across the table. It's because of the gap in my front teeth. Mum says my teeth will grow together one day, but not today. I've got a gap.

Samantha jumps up, crashing her chair to the floor. 'Disgusting, Jack.' Her pigtails are bobbing around like ducks' bums on a pond. 'Mum, Mum, Jack's spitting toast.'

'Sorry, sorry. Didn't mean it.' I point to my gappy front teeth. Samantha screws up her nose in disgust, but I can see she believes me. I start wiping away the toasty bits from the table.

Mum shakes her head and continues squeezing orange juice with Rob's super juicer. Well, it's not that super. It is hard yellow plastic with a spout and a squisher knob that you turn the orange on. Mum gives a huge thump to the orange and accidentally propels a pip into Samantha's head.

'Hey, watch out,' Samantha squeaks.

Poor Samantha. Looks like she is in for a rotten day. I shove Mum. 'Move over.' I grab the squisher. I am not bad at making orange juice. Not too many pips and lumpy bits. But to be honest, Rob is better at it than me.

'Thank you, Jack.' Mum is smiling. That is a good sign. Mum takes a glass of orange juice and I start talking about the Gold Coast. Mum's eyes light up, and in between mouthfuls of juice she blurts out how happy Nanna is about the holiday. Nanna. I forgot Nanna. There are only five seats in the car and Nanna has got wobblier and rounder lately. It's all the chocolate chip cookies she keeps eating, but you can't stop Nanna when there are cookies around.

Nanna. She'll hardly squash in between Samantha and me in the back seat of Mum's old car. Anna won't fit. Puss wanders past, then rubs her back against my leg. I tickle under her chin. Puss purrs. Puss. Wow, Puss — you've given me a great idea. Nanna won't mind if we leave her at home to mind Puss. Someone has to do it. Puss and Nanna. They'll like being together. The Napolis will keep an eye on Nanna as well, so Mum won't have to worry. This is all working out.

I follow Mum into the kitchen and start telling her that Nanna would love to stay home. Oh no, my coffee table. I trip on its wobbly leg and land on my knees, staring at a photo of Nanna. Her face is a huge smile under a yellow straw sun hat. She is standing beside Grandad's grave. Suddenly this sinking, rotten feeling forms a lump in the bottom of my stomach. Nanna misses Grandad a lot. I rub my head. She would miss us too if we went on holidays. No. Nanna wouldn't like to stay home, even with Puss. I finish my orange juice. I can't ask about Anna.

Breakfast over. Mum bounds out of her chair and heads for the kitchen sink. 'What about the dishes?' she sings.

'Dishes?' I moan. 'Dishes? Sure, sure Mum.' I take two plates and slide them into the sink.

Holidays. I will buy something terrific for Anna from the Gold Coast. She will like that. I start to exit the kitchen. Well, nearly. Samantha is clutching my T-shirt with her two grubby fists. I am dragged to a grinding halt. 'Hey, get your paws off my shirt.' Get it? Paws. Dogs. I am thinking of being a stand-up comic when I leave school. 'Let go of my shirt.'

'What about the rest of the dishes on the table? You NEVER clear the table or ever wash up.' Samantha stamps her foot.

'I do. Anyway, that's why Rob is here. It's his job.'

'It's not his job,' Mum puts her hands on her hips.

'He is a great dish washer, Mum. Maybe even the best dish washer in the world.' Mum loves it when I tell her that Rob is a great person. It is so obvious that Mum wants him to be our dad. Samantha always says that Rob is her Dad. It's dumb. We have never had a dad before and we don't need one now.

'Rob does make the glasses sparkle.' Mum gets this dog-eared smile across her face. (See? I am a great comedian, even when I'm not in the mood. I have to think of more dog jokes.)

'But Rob isn't here to wash up.' Samantha stands with her arms crossed. 'And Jack left a disgusting plate covered in tomato sauce in MY bedroom. It smelt awful.'

Mum's blonde fuzz is frizzling. Lately she has been getting a bit wacky about tidiness. She has been nagging me about my room. How can she expect me to keep fungus and living organisms in neat rows? Also, I can't see the point of emptying my waste paper basket every day. That is why I have two waste paper baskets and a cardboard box next to them for the overflow. I think Mum is trying to impress Rob, which is very unfair, since I was here first.

Rob is a tidy freak, except when he leaves his shoes in the lounge room. Mum gets so mad when he does that. But mostly he is a tidy freak, which is one of the dumb things about him. He irons his shirts for hours and thinks my school shirts and even my T-shirts should be ironed. Mum NEVER irons. We have always been the crushed kids and I like it that way. Rob says that I am old enough to iron my own shirts. As if that's right. Rob even irons his handkerchiefs. Now, how stupid is that?

'Jack, you have to clean up after yourself.'

I feel my prickly short hair stand up like a porcupine. 'But I do, Mum.'

Mum takes a daisy from the vase on the table. She puts it behind her ear. Flowers bring peace according to Mum. Peace is Mum's favourite topic. Samantha says she loves flowers too. She always copies Mum. I don't. I'm grafting a daisy onto a tomato vine at the moment. I could be the creator of an edible daisy. That would be something.

Mum runs the sponge over the last dirty plate. 'Done.' She looks at me in this Mum-disappointed way. It's like watching a poppy wilt. I hate that look, and I DO help with the dishes. (Sometimes.)

'I'll clear the table next time,' I mumble.

Samantha hugs Mum. 'I really liked my egg.' Mum takes the daisy from behind her ear and fixes it into Samantha's hair. Samantha heads for the window. 'Nanna should be here soon.' Nanna always comes over on Saturday morning. Samantha presses her nose against the pane, waiting until she sees her. Quickly, she pushes the window up and shouts out of the window, 'Nanna. Nanna.' I don't know why Samantha is shouting. Nanna can't hear, even though Nanna thinks she can. I rush over to see what's happening.

Nanna is outside the Napolis' Super Delicioso Fruitologist Market. She is leaning on her black walking stick. The doctor told her that she has to use it. Nanna pretends to forget to take it when she goes out, but I know it's a lie. She just doesn't want to.

Mr Napoli wanders out of his fruitologist market rubbing a red apple. When he sees Nanna, he starts singing very loudly in Italian. I can just hear him. 'Buon giorno, bella Nonna.' That means 'Good morning, beautiful Grandma.' Mr Napoli is like that. I wonder if all Italians sing. Must ask Anna. Mr Napoli always compliments Nanna on her hair. Nanna loves that. She goes every week to the hairdresser, so that her hair is a hard puffed ball. No one else is allowed to touch her hair in case they mess it up.

Mr Napoli hands Nanna the red apple, which she puts into her bag. She'll probably give it to Mum. Nanna can't eat apples any more. Too tricky, with her false teeth. She has had two teeth missing and a big crack in her front tooth ever since her teeth fell out and slid under the kitchen table. Mum wants

15

her to fix the crack, but Nanna doesn't. 'Now, if you could give me my old teeth back, then I'd get them fixed.' Nanna misses her real teeth. She is always telling us to brush ours, 'otherwise they'll drop out and you won't be able to eat hard caramels'. Nanna would love to eat hard caramels.

'Going to help Nanna come upstairs,' I shout to Mum as I race through the lounge room. 'Come on, Samantha. Stop mucking around.' Samantha gives me a smudgy look, then dashes through the front door just before I slam it shut.

'Don't slam the door,' Mum calls out. Too late.

I race to the fifth step, then do a mighty leap. Success. Second floor landing. Another mighty leap. First floor landing. 'Seven steps in one go. A record!' I yell out to Samantha to move.

'I'll get to the bottom before you,' she laughs. I can't jump because Samantha is in the way. I run down the steps after her, but she is fast and sneaky. 'Beat you.' She giggles and sticks out her tongue.

I chase her down the driveway and past our block of units, and grab her right in front of the Napolis' Super Delicioso Fruitologist Market. 'Got you.' This is a great tickle opportunity. It 'drives Samantha crazy.

'Stop, stop. I give up . . . ha, ha . . . no tickling . . . ha, ha.'

Anna bounds out from inside the fruitologist market and tries to grab my arm. 'Stop tickling her,

Jack.' But I'm too fast and she is not strong enough to keep hold. I tickle and tickle Samantha until she begs for mercy and promises to take my dishes to the kitchen sink every breakfast.

Mr Napoli pats Nanna's arm. His eyes crinkle into a smile. 'You know how boys are.'

Nanna doesn't have a chance to answer because Anna butts in. 'Papa, that is so unfair. It's not boys. It's Jack.' She stamps her foot. 'You're sexist.'

Mr Napoli's moustache quivers. 'Sexist, is this?'

'Yes, Papa.' His moustache is still quivering. Anna stamps her foot again. Her long curly black hair springs down her back as she tosses a look at me.

Anna has amazing licorice twirl hair. She doesn't like it because she thinks it's messy and too curly. I don't think that at all. I watch her dark eyes cannonball at her father until he puts his arms around her. Then her eyes soften into chocolate drops.

'We're going to the Gold Coast for holidays,' I tell Mr Napoli and Anna.

'You'll have so much fun.' Anna's chocolate eyes shine.

Anna is like that. She is really happy for us. We spend ages talking about the theme parks and water slides. Suddenly a gurgling burp pops inside me. Hunger. This is no time to talk. I pat my stomach. 'Mum always cooks something good on Saturdays.' I look at Mr Napoli. 'Can Anna come over? We can check out Mum's cooking.'

'You've just eaten, Jack,' Samantha pipes in. What would she know?

'A boy has to eat.' Mr Napoli smiles at Anna. 'A girl too. See, I am not this sexist. Just go and have a good time, Anna.'

Anna and I walk ahead. 'I wish you could come on holidays with us, but there's not enough room in the car.'

'That's sweet of you to think of me, Jack.'

'That's okay.' I feel my face getting hot. 'We're staying at Port Macquarie on the way up.' I scratch my ear thinking. 'Leo lives there. We're going to see him. Why do you think Rob didn't talk about him before?'

'Maybe Rob wanted to be part of your family first.' Anna speaks seriously.

'Wonder what Leo is like.'

'He'll be nice.'

'Maybe.'

'Rob is his dad, so he has to be.'

'I guess.' I get this choking feeling inside. My father has never even phoned me.

We stop to let Samantha and Nanna catch up. Samantha is holding Nanna's sore hand. It's the arthritis. But her hands weren't always like that. Nanna used to be a great sewer. I suddenly smile. When I was three, she made me a Superman shirt with a red cape. I'd whizz around thinking I could fly. Ha, ha, Flying Jack. Nanna doesn't sew any more.

Nanna arrives at last, then stops. 'I've bought something special for you.'

Oh, this looks interesting. Nanna is definitely the world's best bargain hunter and specials buyer. I like it when she buys cherries and doughnuts. The trouble is that she really, truly likes buying socks and underpants. Lots of them, especially if they are cheap.

'What do you think I've bought?'

'Cookies.' Samantha gives a know-all grin.

'Chocolate chip cookies.' Nanna smiles at Anna. 'I bought an extra one just for you, Anna. And there's something else.' Nanna passes Samantha her walking stick and digs deep inside her bag. There is an excited smile on her face. She has found it. Her green eyes twinkle. 'I am so lucky. Your old ones must be worn out by now. I've been into the shop every week for months to see if they have a sale of them.'

Oh, no. Nanna radiates happiness as she holds them up. Right in the middle of the street. One, two, three, four giant-sized pairs of bright fluorescent purple underpants.

Anna and Samantha are laughing. I look up at our third floor window. Mum is watching and swirling around so that her hair is flying into a tizz. Then I see something horrible. The window is wide open. The sunlight pours into it. Everyone can see. Mum's head disappears from view for a second, then it's back, then it disappears, then it's back . . . her hands clap above her head, her feet propel into star jumps.

'Mum, don't.' I glance nervously around. I hope no one I know sees her. I hope it is not hereditary.

Nanna looks up happily at Mum doing star jumps and waves the purple underpants like a flag.

Chapter 3

Hector the Rat

Samantha is already at the top landing. Anna is behind me. I am behind Nanna in case she slips backwards. I wait and wait as she wobbles onto every step. She is so SLOW. I want to shout at her to MOVE, but I just grit my teeth. She holds on to the handrail like glue. At last she makes it.

'Let's go in, Nanna. Let's go in.' Nanna raises her hand, gulping small puffs of air. Her face crinkles like a bulldog's. Her pink tongue flickers between her teeth. (Dog joke.) She looks funny, snatching short breaths. I start laughing until Anna elbows me in the back. We wait, wait, then wait some more.

At last Nanna is on the move again. She shuffles forward and nearly trips. As I grab her arm, I look down at her black lace-up orthopaedic shoes. I

shudder. They must be hot. Nanna used to wear
sandals. She could run in them. I liked it when
Nanna could run. Run? Even walking would be
great. I take her knobby hand. She squeezes my
fingers softly. Suddenly a throb pounds through my
head. When did Nanna get so old?

Her bum wobbles as she shuffles excitedly
towards the front door. She is desperate to show
Mum her super bargain — four pairs of purple
fluorescent underpants.

Mum has left the door open for us. She isn't star
jumping any more. No, she is waving her old

wooden spoon in the air like she is conducting a symphony orchestra. Music from the radio is blaring through the lounge room and Mum is singing. She sounds awful. 'Mum, stop,' I call out. Anna is too polite to say anything. Mum shouldn't sing. It is like nails scraping down a blackboard, but Mum doesn't GET IT. Nanna thinks Mum sounds lovely because Mum used to sing in the children's choir. That was a LONG time ago. Also Nanna is half-deaf.

Mum just laughs. She thinks we are kidding. 'We're having my famous quiche today.' Mum is very proud of her famous 'melt-in-your-mouth' tomato, cheese, bacon and egg quiche. 'It's for lunch.' Mum twirls around to the music.

I snatch an apple from the fruit bowl. That should stop my stomach's hunger growls. 'Come on,' I say to Anna, pointing to my room. 'Before Mum starts star jumping again.' I grab Samantha's long black checked sausage-dog door stopper on the way.

'Hey, what are you doing with my sausage dog?' Samantha is very protective about her super-tidy room.

'Need it to stop Mum's voice sneaking under the door and blasting into my bedroom.'

Samantha starts to object until Mum begins singing 'Help'. The Beatles didn't realise the damage they were doing when they wrote that song. Help is right. We need it. Anna and Samantha run after me into my room, then I wedge the sausage dog against the door. I turn on the radio. Relief.

Everyone says hello to Hector, my experimental white rat. I got him last birthday after two weeks of begging. Mum doesn't like rats — not that she would hurt them, but she didn't want Hector. It was desperate. A life and death situation. The pet shop owner said that no one wanted Hector and that he was too old to sell. I could have Hector for FREE, otherwise he was going to flush Hector down the drain. When I told Mum, she took the daisy from her hair and smelt it, but I saw her bottom lip trembling. So Hector moved in.

Samantha opens the cage. 'You're cute, Hector.' She crouches down to pat him.

'He's not a dog, Samantha. Ha, ha.' As she gets up she bumps my collection of snakes and bugs. 'Watch out, Clumsy.'

'I'm not clumsy.' She turns up her nose at me. 'What do you expect? Your room is a mess.'

'Yeah, right.' I shove my books about scorpions to the side of my desk. I will need them tonight to finish my homework. Why do teachers have to ruin your life with homework? I look at Anna. 'Hey, make yourself at home.'

Anna is shaking her head. She starts to huff and puff and her lips pucker into a whinge. 'How can you live like this?' She picks up some of my clothes from the floor.

'Hey, leave my stuff alone. That's for the washing basket.'

'Well, why don't you put it INSIDE the basket?'

Samantha is laughing. Anna's chocolate drop eyes have changed to bullet-size ammunition. She is firing at me. 'I can't sit anywhere.' She shoves my clothes off my bed. They flop onto the carpet and land on my camera.

'Watch out.' I grab my camera. I need it to record developments in my important experiments.

Anna just ignores me. 'Now I have somewhere to sit.'

Samantha has this grin on her face as she plunks herself next to Anna. They are staring at each other, nodding in agreement. I hate that. As if tidying my bedroom matters. Did they ever make a ponto? My famous half-onion, half-potato vegetable? (I've been trying to make another ponto ever since my first success, but no luck yet.) Can they make an edible daisy? (Or a nearly edible daisy, anyway.) No way. I look at Anna. Her nose is squished into this disgusted look. It's only the smell of the fungus.

I feel my prickly hair get pricklier. I am getting angry. This is MY room. I start telling them to get out, when I notice Anna's cute dimples. She hates her dimples, but I don't. 'Jack, you should tidy your . . .'

What? I shake my head hard. Anna is talking about emptying the waste paper basket and putting away my clothes. Then she points to my fungus. This is moving towards a disaster. I have no choice but to fight back, even if Anna has cute dimples. Think, Jack, think. I need ammunition. A joke, a joke.

'Hey, I've got a gag.' Anna stops her 'helpful' advice. Samantha wants to hear the gag. She loves my humour, except when it's about her. 'Why did the sausage dog wear sunglasses?'

Samantha's cheeks go red, which means she is thinking. 'The sausage dog wore sunglasses because . . . hmm . . .'

I look at them. They shake their heads. 'Okay, give up?' They think for a bit longer.

'What's the answer?' Samantha twirls her pigtails.

'So as not to be recognised.'

Samantha sniffs. 'That's a bit funny.'

Anna tosses a pillow at me. 'Funny.'

I toss the pillow back at her. Then Samantha throws a pillow and it's on. Blankets, pillows, sheets fly through the air, dropping like nose-diving pigeons. Anna flings a sheet over my head and sits on me. Samantha copies her until I'm lying in a heap on the floor laughing. 'Enough, enough,' I splutter.

'Any more jokes?' Anna's dark curls ripple over me and a tingle spreads through me like bubbles up my nose.

'No, no, no more.' Not for now, anyway.

I help Anna and Samantha make my bed. Crinkle-free blankets. It is the best I have ever seen it, except when Mum does one of her rare mega-cleans. 'Great job,' I tell them.

'You should always keep your bed like this.'

No lectures. I think fast and sidetrack Anna, pointing to my scientific work. She is interested. There is research about sharks and cane toads spread out on my desk. I really want to bring back a cane toad from the Gold Coast. There is a plague of them up there. Interesting stuff. Anna is looking at my jars and beakers. I have had plenty of disappointments. Dead daisies. Dead tomato vines. Dead pontos. Decaying life forms. But that is the way it is with scientists. You have to keep working on new methods and techniques.

Samantha is scrunching up her lips at the dead life forms when Mum opens my bedroom door. 'Rob's here and it's lunch time. Well, quiche time.' Mum laughs because she thinks she is hilarious. Mum will never make a great comedian, but I can't tell her that. It would hurt her feelings.

Rob. I need to ask him if he can get some big bolts, so that I can screw two brackets under my window sill. There is not enough space for all my bottles on the sill any more.

Rob is giving Mum a hug. 'Rob,' I call out. He is carrying two shelves and bolts. 'For me? Are those for me?'

Rob smiles. 'Yes, for you. These should be the right size.'

'How did you know that I needed them? I really do.'

'A scientist has to have room for his work.' He pretends to thump my arm. 'We'll put it up together after lunch. All right?'

Rob has his tools all organised in neat rows in the garage. 'Will we use your hammer drill with a masonry bit?'

'Sounds right, Jack.'

This is so good. I take the shelves and bolts into my room. By the time I am back in the lounge room, everyone is crammed around the dining table. I squish in next to Anna. She smells like peppermint. I like peppermint.

Quiche arrives on the table. Nanna is only having a small piece because she brought cookies and doesn't want to spoil her appetite. Rob and I have the biggest slices. Anna says that she really likes the quiche. Mum beams, because she loves compliments.

The phone rings. It keeps ringing and ringing. Anna raises her eyebrows at me. Conversation stops dead. No one dares pick it up because of Mum's law — her the-phone-is-never-to-disturb-the-family-meal law. Once I picked up the phone in the middle of spaghetti bolognaise. Mum went bright red. Steam looked like it was coming out of her ears. It was horrible. 'They'll phone back if they really want to talk to you,' she said to me. 'This is family time.' Mum is so serious about this rule. There could be an earthquake or a tidal wave, or a giant octopus could be taking over the world, but no, we can never, ever, pick up that receiver.

We are sitting like stuffed dummies waiting for the phone to stop when Rob gets up. 'Could be Leo,' he mumbles. 'Exception. You understand,' he apologises to Mum, then takes the handset into the bedroom.

Mum doesn't explode. She doesn't even get a tiny bit angry. 'Why?' I mouth to Samantha. She shakes her head and pulls one pigtail hard. But NO ONE I have ever known has broken the phone rule. Nanna stops eating her cookie for a second. Anna shakes her head, because she knows Mum's rule too. This is BIG.

Suddenly Rob sticks his head out of the room. 'Leo wants to say hello to Jack and Samantha.'

'Mum?' I look at her.

'Please, Jack,' she says under her breath. 'It's a special situation.'

Special? Unfair, more like it. Is Leo that important? I push back my chair. What am I supposed to talk about anyway? The weather? 'Right, okay. I've got the phone, Rob. Hi, Leo. Yes, it's sunny down here.' Phew. Who can believe this? Saved by the weather. 'Sunny at Port too? That's good.' Hmmm. 'It'll be great to meet when we're up there.' Don't know about that. 'Here, Samantha.' I hand her the receiver. That was so boring.

Oh no, Samantha is talking to Leo about her dog project. BAD NEWS. Rob is smiling. Has he lost his mind? Samantha gives Rob the phone and goes back to the table. The DOG PROJECT.

I shuffle back to the table too. My head is throbbing. I don't get why the phone rule was broken.

Nanna is already looking at the dog project in between mouthfuls of food. I close my left eye so that I can't see Nanna's teeth sliding in and out. Samantha is reading everything aloud. Five whole minutes pass of Samantha's dog talk and Nanna's teeth sliding in and out. My stomach is turning. I thump my watch. Nanna gulps and her teeth get stuck inside her mouth. Good. But Samantha doesn't stop. Bad. I have to do something NOW.

I scrape back my chair with a long screechy tear-your-eardrum-out sound. Samantha keeps reading. I crash my fork on my plate and nearly crack the plate. She keeps reading. I yawn loudly for at least ten seconds. She looks up, then gives me one of her famous don't-you-dare-disturb-me-again stares. She looks like a zombie. I am not going to get her to shut up. I give up.

Anna is squishing against my arm. Suddenly flushes start to track up the sides of my nose. Anna asks if I'm all right and touches my hand. I feel the red spread out across my face to my ears. My arms are crawly with goosebumps. What is wrong with me? An allergy, probably.

'The assignment is wonderful, darling,' Mum says as Samantha finally closes it. Mum is crazy.

Nanna has cookie sludge stuck in the front of her false teeth. It is brown and squelchy. Yuck. I look at Rob finishing his orange juice. He throws the newspaper onto the couch. 'Terrorist attacks.' He scratches his prickly head.

'Terrorism.' Mum sighs. Oh, I can see her eyes cloud over. It must mean the start of one of Mum's talks. She picks up a photo from the wobbly coffee table. It is the one I took of her with a 'Make Love Not War' poster at last year's International Women's Day. Samantha is in the picture too, doing a handstand and eating a drippy meat pie upside down. Great photograph. Next to it, there is a small one of Mum wearing a flower-power dress. My father used to be next to her, but he has been cut away. No one knows where my father is.

'It's about hate.' Oh, is Mum still talking about it? Hate. For ages I hated my father because he left us and because Mum hated him. She changed her mind later because 'He gave me you kids. Nothing is better than that.' Mum says that hating eats a hole inside you, so that you always hurt.

Hate? I don't hate my father now, because he is nobody to me. A sad feeling quickly comes, then goes. I have Rob. I shake my head. I really know what hate is, though. A big picture of George Hamel looms into my head. Dumb idiot. He made my life rotten last year. 'Bum Head' is what he called me. I don't hate George Hamel any more. He can't hurt me any more. I've got friends and other things to think about. Anna flashes into my mind, then Leo. A chill runs down my back.

The terrorism talk is over. I don't like thinking about it. The world makes me feel unsafe sometimes, but then I have my family. I'm lucky.

Mum is hugging Samantha. Rob stands and stretches his legs. Washing up duty. He always moans when he does the washing up, but he is just faking it. He likes washing up. We have to clear the table or he gets really angry. I sometimes help with the dishes, but it is really Rob territory. He prepares the detergent and scrubbing brush and makes the water HOT. He doesn't even wear rubber washing-up gloves.

Mum admires the sparkling dishes. The plates are amazing. You need sunglasses to look at them. Mum starts talking about the holiday. I look at Anna. Wish she could come. Then I look at Nanna. Oh, well. Hey, Anna and Nanna rhyme. I never realised that before. I'll think up a clever joke about that.

'We're staying in an apartment on the Gold Coast. Right across from the beach. It'll be lovely.' Mum gets this glow over her face. I'm not sure if it's because of Rob's washing up or the beach.

I ignore Mum's gooey-ness. Have to get to the facts. 'How many bedrooms?' I cross my fingers. I don't want to share a room with Nanna. She snores.

'Everyone will be there.' Well, I know that already. 'There will be a room for Nanna.' Yippee. 'Another for Rob and me. There is an alcove for Samantha.' Mum twirls her hair into a knot. 'And another room for the boys.'

Boys? I laugh. 'There's only ONE boy here, Mum.'

Mum hesitates, looks at Rob. He puts his arm around her. 'We're collecting Leo at Port Macquarie,' she says.

Rob smiles. 'Haven't seen him for a while. He'll like a holiday.'

Why is Rob smiling? Leo? What? Rob just announces that Leo is coming with us to the Gold Coast for the whole holiday.

Mum looks at Samantha. 'We'll have a bigger family.'

Family? I don't even know Leo. This is too fast. Samantha is elbowing me. I roll my eyes at her. Rob is watching both of us. I try to smile. How can Leo fit in the car? Nanna will have to stay home after all. Poor Nanna. No holidays for Nanna. This is bad.

I knew Rob shouldn't have moved in with us.

Chapter 4

Scorpions and Garbage Fights

Mum tries to tell us that having Leo on our holiday will be fun. At the end of a ten-minute lecture on all the reasons why Leo is a great addition to our family, she suddenly stops. 'You're not listening, are you?' But she isn't angry when she says that.

'We are, Mum,' Samantha hugs her. 'You want us to like Leo a lot, Mum. A real lot.'

I groan. 'Yes, a real lot.'

Mum smiles. 'You kids see right through me, don't you?' She waits for a second, then looks at us. 'I'm not being honest, am I?'

I shrug. What am I supposed to say? She's been different since Rob, and even worse since Leo.

'We all have to get used to each other. Sometimes it's going to be hard.' Mum takes the daisy from behind her ear and holds it. Suddenly out of nowhere she adds, 'Leo is twelve like you two, Jack and Anna.'

'Yes, Mum.' Samantha nods.

Anna and I smile at each other, because Mum is like that. She just drops random things into the middle of a conversation.

Mum gives us money and tells us to go down to the beach and buy ice creams. As we all climb down the stairs, Anna says, 'It will be okay with Leo.'

'I've never met Leo. Funny name.' I shake Mum's talk out of my head. 'Let's hurry up.' Of course, they are slow. 'Right, you're on,' I roar like a lion, then start chasing them down the street. 'Leo the lion coming. Leo the lion.'

We're all panting by the time we reach the shop. Mr Green knows us. Anna buys a butterscotch ice cream. Samantha gets caramel, of course. Mango for me. We are licking, dripping ice cream. Samantha looks like she has a caramel beard. Luckily we've got an ocean where we can wash it off. We go to investigate the sea pools on the rock platform at the edge of the beach. Samantha finds a red starfish at the bottom of one of the pools. I find a jellyfish. 'Jellyfish,' I shout out. They know the game and start running.

'Stop it, stop it.' Samantha laughs. 'No chasing.'

But I am in a chasing mood. The girls start sprinting, with me charging behind them. 'Jellyfish, jellyfish. Tentacles will suck out your eyes.' I chase them all the way to the cliffs at the far end of the beach.

I don't suck out their eyes, but we climb the cliffs and find our favourite boulder. There is a ship right out at sea. We sit on the edge of the boulder and dangle our legs over it. I like the smell of the ocean spray and the noise of the crashing waves.

We wander back along the beach, shake the sand from between our toes. I jiggle my pocket. Yes, there is enough money left for chewing gum. We reach Mr Green's shop and insert money into the gum ball machine. Anna blows a huge red bubble. Samantha copies, but her tongue always gets in the way. My bubble isn't bad. It's blue. We blow bubbles all the way home.

I bang on our front door. Mum opens it. 'Hi, Mum. Hi, Nanna. Hi, Rob.'

Rob is standing with his hands in his pockets and leaning against the window. Was he on the look-out for us?

'We're here,' I announce.

Rob smiles. I think he was waiting for us. 'Now, I'm not sure if anyone is ready for this.'

Hope this isn't another you-will-like-Leo lecture. Leo probably has two heads and a tail. I smile. At least that would make him a good scientific study.

'I've got something downstairs that you all might like. For our holiday.'

Yep, it's probably a lion-taming harness for Leo. It will need to have two head braces. I stare at my feet. If I look at Rob, I'll start laughing.

'What, Rob? What?' Samantha runs up to him.

Rob usually has something interesting to show us. He brought home a second-hand surfboard last month. It had a few dings in it but Rob and I patched it up. Rob also likes thermometers. Lots of thermometers. There is one in every room so that we know the temperature variations in every place in our unit. It is much hotter in the lounge room with the afternoon sun. The coolest place is Samantha's bedroom. She's lucky in summer. I like thermometers too.

Samantha begs Rob to tell us what the surprise is, but Rob is not telling. Samantha grabs his hand and starts pulling him to the door. She's too weak. No muscles. But I have plenty of muscles, so I join in and so do Anna and Mum. I can see out of the corner of my eye that Nanna wants to push too, but she would topple over. So she just holds Puss to make sure that we don't squash her as we drag Rob out of the unit.

'Hey, I'm being captured. Stop, stop.' Rob is laughing, but we don't stop. We push him onto the landing and down the first set of stairs, then the next, then the next, until we are right outside. 'All right, all right. Let go of me or I won't show you what I've got.'

'Can we trust you?' I keep my hold on him, but Samantha, Anna and Mum have already let go. Typical.

Rob sticks his finger into Samantha's stomach, making her giggle. 'Follow me.' We follow in line along the driveway into the backyard. Everyone keeps asking questions, but Rob won't give the answer away.

There is nothing in the backyard except the usual. A few cars parked in the car park, the grassy yard, the basketball ring. 'So what is it?'

'Look very hard.' Rob is enjoying this. Mum hits him on the arm. Samantha copies Mum, of course. 'All right, all right, you dictators.' He gets this sad doggy-faced look. (Note the dog joke.) 'I give up. Defeated, that's me.' He walks slowly over to a silver four-wheel-drive Land Rover with shiny chrome bull bars. He gives us a last look, then smiles. 'Come on, everyone.' We stare at him. What is he doing? 'Kids, get in.'

'What?'

'It's ours.'

'Ours?' Shock makes me speechless.

Samantha is squealing, since she is never speechless. She starts to jump up and down like a bouncing rubber ball. Mum sneaks a look at Rob. She has known about this all along for sure.

'Okay, okay.' Rob gets into the driver's seat. 'Get in now. Let's take it for a spin.'

Crashes, girl giggles, we are in. This is some car. I can smell the newness of it. The seats are so comfortable. Wow. Rob drives slowly past Nanna, whose head is sticking out of our third floor window. We wave and shout. Nanna waves back. Then Rob drives past the Napolis' Super Delicioso Fruitology Market. The Napolis call out as Rob beeps the horn. Then Rob drives into the main street, over the bridge near our school, and around three roundabouts and two parks. Mum is hugging Rob's arm even though he is driving. We have never, ever, ever, had a new car. And we have never had a car like this.

I look around. I think about Anna and Nanna. There are SEVEN seats. Enough room for Nanna and Anna, as well as Leo. All of us. It doesn't take any persuading at all for both Mum and Rob to agree. Anna is allowed to come with us on holiday. Yessss!!!

Anna's face dimples when I ask her. 'Holidays. I'd like that.' Then she stammers, pressing her lips together. She stumbles over the words. 'I may not be allowed. You know Papa.'

'We'll persuade him, Anna.' I give a confident look and Anna smiles, but I'm not that sure. It's because Mr Napoli is traditional. That means he sings Italian songs, eats pasta, tells jokes that aren't funny, works hard and is very strict. He worries about Anna. He would worry about road accidents on the long drive up the coast. He would worry about sharks in tropical waters. He would worry about Anna staying up too late at night.

I get help. Mrs Napoli and Mum talk and talk to Mr Napoli. I'd get a headache if I was him. Mum tries to describe all the safety parts of Rob's four-wheel drive. It is pathetic. I have to interrupt. Mum knows NOTHING about cars except that you have to put petrol in them and call road service when you have a flat tyre. I explain important technical features like the 4.1 litre engine, huge mag wheels, reserve petrol tank, wrap-around bull bars. But in the end, it is Mrs Napoli who persuades him. She whispers something in his ear that makes his moustache jiggle.

Mum shoves her elbow into my side. 'How romantic. It'll be just them.' I stare at Mr Napoli. 'Love birds for a week.' At this point, I have to leave. I don't want to hear any more. Mr and Mrs Napoli as lovebirds is a horrible thought.

Next morning. Last day of term. The sun is shining and I am smiling. I grab my scorpion assignment. I stayed up all night finishing it. Scorpions are incredible. It is hard to believe that those bugs have such huge stings in their tails. There is one giant-sized type of scorpion that lives in the deserts of

America. It is long, hairy and about twelve centimetres long. When I told Rob that last night, he made some disgustingly rude jokes. He never makes those jokes in front of Mum. It is male stuff. I flash my INTERESTING project (not DOGS) at Samantha. 'Some scorpions can hurt you.' I give Samantha a hardly-sting-you pinch. 'Like that, but worse. Much worse.'

Samantha hits me hard. 'Don't.' She rubs her arm.

As if that hurts. I ignore her whingeing and go on. 'There is one scorpion in California that bites you and makes you froth at the mouth as you twitch and convulse to death.'

'I don't want to hear any more.'

But I want to show her more. Samantha squeals when I wave a really big, gigantic picture of a scorpion in front of her. The more she squeals, the more I flash pictures of scary-hairy creepy-crawlies. It's fun.

I glance out of my bedroom window and notice Anna waiting for us outside the Napolis' Super Delicioso Fruitology Market. I put away the scorpion project. Anna mightn't like it. Next term we are doing the Amazon River. That means piranhas. Now, that is a really great topic. I've read that red-bellied piranhas can eat a whole man alive.

I stick my head out of the window and Anna waves her cap at us. The sun streams through her dark hair, flecking it with diamonds.

'Let's go, Samantha.' We shout goodbye to Mum and race down the stairs.

Mrs Napoli must have seen us, because she comes out of the Super Delicioso Fruitology Market with three yellow mangoes. 'Beautiful. Juicy. For your lunch.' She hands us a mango each, then kisses Anna goodbye.

The school bus is full of kids. 'Hey, Christopher,' I call out. He is blowing a big red bubble at me. It bursts all over his face. Samantha slides in between the bus railing and the driver's seat. She has been getting taller and less chubby since she turned eleven. Anna pushes down the aisle towards her friends. They squish together on their seat to make room for her. 'Rub-a-dub-dub. Three babes in a tub,' I shout out over the heads of everyone. There is laughing and Anna shakes her head at me.

'Just kidding,' I shout out again.

'You're not amusing,' one of the girls calls out in this exaggerated voice.

The bus suddenly jerks forward, setting off a tidal wave of kids crashing into each other. George Hamel is at the back of the bus. He is being hammered by waves of squashed kids. He doesn't even move to the side to get less squashed. He is a real meathead. Hamburger for brains. I wish his muscles were hamburger too. He is built like a truck. I don't get into arguments with him any more, not after last year when he nearly flattened me. But I will stand up to him now if I have to. These days he leaves me alone. I leave him alone too. It's all good.

The bus slams to a stop outside school. There is racing and shoving. I have to protect my scorpion assignment from the crush, and my mango as well. I stick my hand in my bag. No squashed mango. Phew.

Anna and Samantha head inside the school grounds. I run towards my classroom to check if my teacher is there. Yes, he is working at his desk. I charge through the door, waving my scorpion assignment. He looks up at me. Points to his watch. 'Last minute, I see.' I put the assignment on his desk just as the school bell rings. Made it.

Last day of term is always tidy-up mania day. Teachers run around with dusters and buckets and force kids to wipe, polish, mop. Desks are scrubbed clean of sticky stuff. White boards wiped super clean. Gum scraped off the bottoms of chairs. Playing fields cleared of even a trace of rubbish — no old apple cores or empty cans or lunch wrappers.

George Hamel starts a garbage fight in the playing fields. It is like an air raid, with bomber oranges and tomato shrapnel locking into crazy skirmishes. I propel a banana skin into a helicopter spin. It is terrific until it splats at George Hamel's feet. There's cheering from my friends.

'Great shot.' Christopher thumps me on my back.

George Hamel smirks at me as he chucks my banana skin back into the battle. 'Not a bad throw for a beginner.'

'For sure.' I laugh. My friends laugh with me. A beginner? As if I am. That spin was scientifically worked out. I look at George Hamel and a joke bursts into my brain.

What is the difference between a Hamel and a camel? One has a knob on his back. The other is a knob.

I am laughing under my breath. I want to say it to George Hamel but I don't. Last year George Hamel and his mates hammered me, and everyone else did too. Having a joke with some people is not a great idea. Anyway, everyone saw my throw.

Suddenly Christopher is thumped by a half-eaten orange. He chucks it at Paul. Paul chucks it at me. Yuck, it's slimy. I look around for a good victim to throw it at when the teacher's voice belts over the fields. 'Stop it. NOW.' I keep hold of the orange, but a few missiles are still in mid-flight. The teacher waits until they land. 'One more flying object and the whole lot of you will be staying in after school.' That is a horrible thought. It's the last day of school and no one wants to hang around. Everyone stops immediately.

We have the longest assembly in the world. The Principal drones on and on about keeping the school clean, returning library books, making sure parents sign permission slips for excursions, completing assignments. I watch a fly trying to land on the Principal's head. The Principal rubs his bald patch, scaring that fly right out of the hall. Wish I was a fly. Slowly, slowly his droning ends. He finishes with the best words in the whole assembly. 'Have a great holiday.' There is cheering and clapping.

Goodbye school. Hello holidays. My bag is loaded with junk to take home. Samantha is struggling under her backpack. I throw it over my shoulder. I am in a great brotherly mood. Anna follows me. The bus is chaotic. Last school bus for the term means near-riot. The bus driver is shouting down some kids down the back. 'Sit down, you idiots, or I'll stop the bus.'

An apple hurtles through the air and lands on Paul's lap. 'Great shot,' he yells back.

Our bus stop is next. Samantha presses the bell. It jerks to a halt. 'Bye,' I say to the bus driver. He is usually a nice guy, except on the last day of term. I call out goodbye to the rest of the kids on the bus. I notice another apple fly through the air.

Anna, Samantha and I watch the bus struggle away down the road. We look at each other, then burst out laughing. I throw my bag in the air, do a flying jump and catch it. Samantha cheers. Anna cheers. Freedom for two weeks. YES.

Chapter 5

Bite Your Bum

Packing is two days of manic-panic. Samantha wants to take EVERYTHING in her room. Mum and Samantha have a big argument about it. Rob butts in, and they get mad at him. 'It's none of your business, Rob.' Mum stamps her foot. Rob hardly ever gets upset, but he does this time. He exits into their bedroom and Mum ends up running after him. That means it is serious. My head throbs. I hate it when they argue. I stand outside their half-open door.

Rob is loud, for Rob anyway. 'Am I part of this family?'

'Yes, of course you are,' Mum says.

'Every time I say anything to the kids, you turn on me.'

'I don't mean it.' I can hardly hear Mum. She mumbles something, '. . . sorry . . . sorry.'

'You want me to be their father, or at least their step-father.' He is quiet. 'How can I be, if you don't give me a chance? You want to control everything in the family.'

'I don't. Please, Rob. Give me, give us all a chance,' Mum begs. 'It's hard making a new family. Give us time. This holiday,' she stammers, 'is important. The kids have got a lot to work out. All the kids, including Leo. I'm a bit scared.' My head is pounding now. Leo? Why is Mum scared? 'I just want everything to work.' Mum is rubbing her eyes. Is she crying? What am I supposed to do? Should I go in? I hate it when Mum cries.

I take a deep breath and open the door a little more. What? Mum and Rob are hugging. The throbbing in my head sinks into a dull thud. I close the door.

After they come out, Mum and Rob are a bit quiet to each other for a while. Mum tries to smile as she walks past Rob. He nods at her, then turns to me. 'Right, Jack. Let's put on the roof racks.'

I walk with him to the garage. He takes out the racks and we work together, screwing them into place. 'It's going to be a great holiday, Jack.' He tightens the bolts with a spanner. 'It'll be the whole family with Leo there.'

Leo? Family? I rub my hands down my shirt. They are sweaty. I have never asked Rob about Leo before, even when the photo of him just appeared on the coffee table. I want to ask him. I suck in air. 'Hey, Rob.'

He keeps tightening the bolts. 'What?'

I clear my brain, concentrate. Suddenly I feel nervous and stammer Rob's name again. 'Rob. Rob. Why did you never talk about Leo before?' I take a breath. 'Why did you leave Leo?'

Rob gives a final turn to the bolt. 'That looks right now.' He puts down the spanner, then puts his hand on my shoulder. 'Let's sit outside.' I follow Rob to a grassy spot next to the back of the units. I slide onto the grass and lean against the wall. Rob slides next to me. 'Okay, Jack.' He is quiet. 'You've got a right to know.' He stops again. 'Leo's mother left me for someone else.' He digs the heel of his shoe into the grass, making a hole. 'That was tough. It was even tougher because of the Family Court. She took Leo.' He rubs the stubble on his face. 'Then she moved away up north, to Port Macquarie. It meant I couldn't see Leo much.' Rob looks at me. 'Things are different now, though. I hope you are going to be friends.' He pushes back the grass over the hole he made. 'I miss him.'

This lump sticks in my throat. Leo is so lucky.

We walk back together. 'Hey, where have you been?' echoes down the stairwell. Samantha's face peers over the railing.

'Coming,' Rob calls back.

'Hurry up.' Samantha's face disappears.

There is last-minute packing still going on. Mum is a whirlwind. Luggage is stacked on the landing. Rob tells Samantha that there is no room in the car for her ballerina quilt, but she is allowed to take Floppy. Samantha begs to take her quilt. Mum disappears into the kitchen and says nothing and Samantha doesn't pack it.

Eventually everyone is ready. Samantha is bringing her CD player and special ballerina pillow. Mum organises survival items like sunscreen, food, towels. Rob and Nanna don't pack very much. Me neither, except for two secret things — my jar of fungus and a tin of orange paint.

I just couldn't leave my fungus at home. It is getting to an interesting stage, turning a bright green with creamy blobs. The famous Australian scientist Howard Florey made penicillin from fungus. I could discover something important too.

The paint is a different thing. Christopher gave it to me. It was left over from the renovations of his parents' Vietnamese bakery. I need it for Port Macquarie. More details later. By the way, Christopher is looking after Hector. I am going to miss my rat.

Roof is loaded. Samantha and Anna are already in the back of the car. Nanna is belted in. I sit in the middle row with an empty seat between Nanna and me. I hold Mum's emergency food hamper on my lap. There are doughnuts from Christopher's bakery (they always give us free doughnuts); ham and cheese wholemeal sandwiches (Mum is into her health kick again and white bread is never to cross our lips until the next time she forgets); apple juice and paper cups (Samantha is into recycling); peaches and strawberries (provided by the Napolis); and Nanna's chocolate chip cookies (delicious).

Rob shouts, 'Has everyone got their seat belts on?' Samantha clicks in. The Napolis hover outside the car windows. They say they will call us on Rob's mobile phone. (The spare parts warehouse gave it to him so they can phone him for emergencies. Rob is important.) Mrs Napoli is holding Puss. Her black fur shines in the sunlight. I wonder if Puss likes pizza. Anna blows a kiss. 'Bye, Papa. Bye, Mamma.' Mrs Napoli is wiping her eyes, and Mr Napoli has his arm around her.

We all wave and shout as we drive away. We look fantastic riding along in Rob's silver four-wheel-drive off-the-road land cruiser. It is worth having Rob as our . . . dad? Step-father? No, I mean driver. He is Leo's dad. I gulp this lump back down my throat.

I stare at the back of Rob's head. His hair is shorter and pricklier than mine. He got it cut especially for the trip. When he arrived home with it, Mum said he looked like a golf ball that had landed in a pine needle forest. Everyone had a great time hassling Rob about golf balls. That reminds me. I haven't hassled for a while. 'How's golf, Rob?'

Rob pretends to be angry and grumbles, 'Right, Jack.'

Mum turns on the radio to the most boring station possible. 'Music to relax to.' Anna clenches her teeth. Samantha begs Mum to change the station. Luckily we eventually get out of the city and the radio doesn't transmit properly. Mum has no choice. She has to turn it off. Relief.

Suddenly Mum starts talking about Leo. 'It'll be nice to have Leo with us.' 'More kids, more fun.' 'Leo plays basketball.'

Rob adds a few extra comments like, 'Leo has an aquarium with tropical fish.'

I pretend to be interested. Well, I am interested in aquariums, but not in Leo's. 'Aquariums are great,' I say. That should make Rob happy. Wish Rob would stop being such a try-hard.

Suddenly Nanna pipes up. 'Jack likes fish.' Oh no, not that fish story. I try to butt in but Nanna is determined. 'When Jack was a baby he swallowed a tropical fish.'

'Nanna, we don't want to hear this.' I turn to look at her. She doesn't really see me. Her eyes are focused somewhere else. Nanna is on a search-and-destroy-Jack mission. She usually forgets everything, but not this.

'We found the poor fish later. Jack pooped it out in his nappy.' Everyone is laughing. 'The fish was green. It was right next to his little pee-pee.'

I hate Nanna. There are splutters from everywhere. I have begged and begged Nanna dozens of times not to tell that story, but she still does. I can't take the laughing, especially Anna's. I shove a tape over Mum's shoulder. Any music is fine. I am not talking to anyone. I want to kill Nanna. The music is playing at last. There are more giggles. Of course, Nanna is already closing her eyes. She must be really exhausted after humiliating me in front of everyone. I hate Nanna.

We're out of the city now. We speed between eucalyptus forests. There are lots of fish and pee-pee comments. I refuse to say a word. The laughing eventually stops. I stare out of the window. Everything is green at first, but it changes. There were fires last month. Huge tracts of bush are burnt orange. Mum points out the black matchstick trees. I ignore her and press my chin into my arm. There is no undergrowth any more, just dirt and tree stumps like skeletons. Wasted land spreads out as far as you can see. Mum and Rob are talking about the bush fires. I remember the news flashes on TV. Wildlife park officers were holding these small scared possums. Their paws and noses were burnt. I overhear Anna say that she hopes the kangaroos raced faster than the flames. I do too.

Australia burns sometimes. When it is too dry and hot and there is that wild wind, the eucalyptus trees suddenly erupt into flames. The fires this time were bad. Firefighters were burnt. Half the fires were deliberately lit. I don't get why people do that.

Rob stops at a highway rest area surrounded by burnt trees. We stretch our legs, have a drink. I stand against a black stump for a while, still trying to calm down about Nanna and the fish story. Nanna is stuck in the car. It's too hard for her to get in and out for just a short stop. She notices me and blows a kiss. She does it three times until I guess I have to forgive her. As I get back into the car, I whisper, 'Nanna, PLEASE don't tell the fish story again.'

She looks surprised. 'Of course not, Jack. Not if you don't want me to.'

I sigh. Nanna will forget that promise. The dumb fish story is stuck in her brain forever.

We are off again. Taped music is on. It's not too bad, even though Samantha chose it. Anna and Samantha start to sing along with the music. Luckily Mum doesn't know the song, and it is pretty good for a while. Then something awful happens. Mum starts la-la-ing in time with the guitars. Anna raises her eyebrows and looks at me for help. I have to do something. What will I do? What? It comes to me in a brilliant flash of genius.

'Mum, let's do limericks.' Mum loves limericks. Her la-la-ing stops. She switches off the tape.

Anna and Samantha yell out together, 'YES.'

I have been working on this limerick ever since I thought of the Anna–Nanna rhyme. It is a good moment to present my masterpiece.

There was once a grandma called Nanna
Who was eating cookies with Anna.
They sat on the floor
And ate twenty-four
But Nanna told Anna, 'We need more.'

Anna hits my arm, but she is giggling, so I know it is a friendly hit. That's good. Nanna chuckles, nearly tottering over. Luckily she has a seat belt on.

Mum's hair is frizzling. She has an idea. 'I've got a limerick. I've got one.' Mum's brain is hot now.

'Limerick,' she splutters, and shakes her hands in the air.

I have a crazy family called Trouble
They fall into one disaster or other
Until they meet Rob
With his hair cut like a log
Who drives them all safely on holidays.

'That is pathetic, Mum.' There are moans and groans from the back seats. Rob of course thinks it is an excellent limerick. He is kidding, but I've started something. Limerick fever. Even Rob makes up one about three blind mice without tails eating cheese.

'That is dumb, dumb, dumb, Rob,' I tell him. The limericks get stupider and stupider until everyone laughs for no reason. When I call out, 'Limerick about fats-wobble', we collapse into a heap, except for Rob of course. He is driving.

'Got to do a wee,' Samantha squeals. 'Urgent.'

'Hold on.' Rob swerves into a dirt clearing, then grinds to a halt. 'Good timing, Samantha. This is our lunch stop.' Limerick fever ends. Lunch. 'O'Sullivan's Rest. Interesting spot here,' Rob says. I look around as I get out of the car. There are huge eucalyptus trees, bush trails into the wilderness, wooden picnic tables and benches, and a track winding towards the toilets. The bush fires didn't get to this spot. Rob is telling the girls a few things about O'Sullivan's Rest. 'I brought Leo here once.'

Leo? That is it. I'm not interested.

'Got to get my camera. Left it in the car.' I look back as I head for the car. Samantha is hugging Rob, even though she says she is desperate for a wee. She can't be that desperate. Samantha lets go of Rob, then puts her arm through Anna's and they set off for the bush track toilets.

'I'm back,' I announce, and snap a photo of Nanna and Mum.

Rob is leaning against the wooden picnic table stretching his legs. 'I needed a break.' He winks at me. 'After all those limericks.' He rubs his chin. 'Especially the "great" limerick about Nanna and Anna.' He is laughing at me.

'What about your stupid limerick about the mouse? It was like old cheese. Stinky!'

Rob laughs again. I got him on that one. He always makes fun of me. I look at Mum. She is talking to Nanna and didn't even hear him. Rob NEVER makes fun of me in front of Mum. He's tricky like that. I'd argue some more, but I have to go to the toilet too.

The girls are already back. Anna races towards us with her licorice curls bouncing. Samantha follows with her caramel pigtails flapping. Joke, joke. 'You both look like lollies.'

'What are you talking about, Jack?' Samantha snubs her nose at me. I hate it when she does that.

I was going to explain my joke but I am bursting. 'Are the toilets okay?'

'They're clean.' Anna smiles.

Samantha is giggling. 'They're cans, Jack. Better watch out for the spiders. Could bite your bum.'

'Funny, funny.' I race towards the toilets. I notice movement up the trunks of some of the trees, but I am in a hurry. Samantha is right. They are cans. Don't feel like peeing in a toilet where there are lots of other pees and poos. No one is looking. I do a whizz behind the toilets on a tree. That's when I see it. A huge reptile with a long thick tail and a head like a snake. It must be nearly two metres long. I stop dead still. Then I notice two others clawed on to a tree trunk. My breathing is pretty heavy now. Then I see a tongue-flicking scaly monster crawling towards me. That is my cue to run fast.

Anna sees me coming and waves. She has no idea. There is an invasion. They are everywhere. I am shouting, pointing back. 'Look, look.' Gasping, I clutch on to the picnic table. 'Stop,' pant, 'look,' pant. We are trapped in some dinosaur time warp. I've got to save everyone. 'Do you see them? Do you? We've got to run. Run . . .' My voice panics into screeching.

'Don't scream, Jack.' Samantha is too stupid to see danger. 'They panic easily. You'll scare them.'

'They've been known to climb people if you give them a fright.' Mum winks at Samantha.

'And they have sharp claws. To grab on to the trees.' Samantha winks back at her.

What are they talking about? Claws? What's wrong with everyone?

'Rob told me that they have two penises as well.' Samantha shakes her head. 'That's amazing, don't you think? It's like a spare in case one doesn't work.'

Penises? Have they lost their brains? Danger. Reptiles. Dinosaurs. Nanna will be too slow to escape. I look at Mum, then Anna, then Samantha. They are smiling. A huge dinosaur is rocking towards our picnic table. No one is moving. I am starting to think this is a set-up.

'They like small rodents. You're too big for them, Jack,' Rob says, looking serious.

What?

Everyone bursts out laughing, even Nanna. It IS a set-up.

They're all doubled over. 'GOANNAS.'

Big stupid lizards. Everyone knows goannas don't hurt you.

Chapter 6

Orange Paint

Two hours in the car before we reach Port Macquarie. Two hours listening to Mum's music (she has found a 1980s radio station). Two hours of goanna jokes (every fifteen minutes). One hour of Nanna snoring (she's fallen asleep). Half an hour of Samantha whingeing, 'How long until we get there?' The only consolation is Anna. 'Don't worry about the goannas. You didn't know. I thought you were brave coming to save us.' A tingle whooshes down my back.

Finally Mum switches off the radio. She turns around to look at us in the back seat. 'Nearly at Port. We'll be collecting Leo soon.' She rests her hand on Rob's shoulder. 'It's going to feel strange at first. Leo doesn't know you and you don't know him. There are three of you, so it's up to you kids to make Leo feel at home.' Mum is blushing. My head feels funny. Everything will be different. I just know it.

'I thought we were picking Leo up tomorrow, Mum.'

'Didn't I tell you? I thought I did.' Mum rubs her hands through her blonde fuzz. 'Sorry, darling. Sorry.'

'Mum,' I groan. She knows she isn't allowed to call me Darling.

'Sorry, darling. No, I don't mean darling. Jack.' Mum is acting weird. 'We'll be collecting Leo soon. It'll be great.' Mum is really blushing now. 'Yes, great.'

Great? Mum is repeating herself. I don't like it. My head hurts.

'There are four of you kids now.' Rob coughs. 'Leo could feel like an outsider. It'd be great if you could make him welcome.'

Great, great, great. I press my hands down on my head to stop it bursting. I look out of the window. As we drive into Port Macquarie I squint, trying to make out the port. There it is. Deep-sea fishing boats are moored behind the seawall. I squint harder. Then I see them. Boulders, thousands of them wedged together to stop the sea from crashing into the inlet. I turn around and give Samantha and Anna a sly look. I am heading out there today.

Rob turns left into an ordinary street. He parks by the side of the road. As he gets out, he tells us to wait. 'I'll be back soon.'

'Take your time,' Mum presses his hand.

Take your time. That's an understatement. We wait and wait and wait. I open the door for air. It's hot.

'Good idea.' Mum opens her door too.

Then we wait some more.

At last, Rob is back. He is carrying a bag and there is Leo walking beside him. He's skinny and wears his cap backwards. No, he doesn't have two heads. I can't help smiling. He looks like the photo on the coffee table. Rob opens the car door. 'This is Leo.' As if we didn't know.

'Hi,' we all say as he squishes in between Nanna and me like peanut butter in a sandwich.

'One big happy family,' Rob announces.

How corny is that?

As Rob drives off, he starts talking. He talks and talks. It is so un-Rob-like. He makes us talk too, answering dumb questions and giving inside information about what we do. 'Leo likes swimming. You kids do too, don't you?' 'Leo is good at computer games. Who else plays the computer? He's brought some games.' 'Jack is a scientist, you know, Leo.' 'Leo is in the same year as you at school, Jack and Anna.' 'Jack made a coffee table.' Blah, blah, blah. 'Leo has an aquarium. Leo likes fish.'

Oh no, not FISH. Did Nanna hear that? She is looking out of the window. Phew. I just couldn't stand a repeat of the fish story, especially in front of Leo. I give Samantha a dirty look. If she mentions fish, she is dead. No, she is too busy talking about her DOG project. Saved by her dog project. Who would believe it?

Rob drives past the look-out. I stretch, trying to get a good view of it. You can see the cliffs running along the coastline for a long way. He veers into the driveway of the holiday house. 'We're here.'

At last. This is a great old wooden house. I like its creaky wooden porch with bright red bougainvillea hanging from it. Got to be careful of those bougainvillea. They have bloodthirsty dagger thorns. I fell into the bougainvillea once when I was taking samples for my edible flower experiments.

Rob parks. I open the door as fast as I can to de-paste myself from Leo. Being stuck next to him is not great fun. I am definitely not sitting next to him in the car tomorrow.

'Minimal luggage tonight. We don't want to be unpacking and then repacking tomorrow.' Rob is in his organising mood. His golf ball head bobs up and down in and out of the car like a broken spring.

I start laughing. 'Hey, Rob, have you taken out your orange juice squisher for breakfast tomorrow?'

His head stops bobbing around and he looks at me, then laughs. He knows he's an organising maniac and there is NO way his squisher would be left at home. 'Funny, Jack.'

'What do you mean?' Leo slides out of the car.

Rob is too busy to hear him. 'It's a private joke,

Leo. Between Rob and me.' Leo scrunches up his face and shrugs.

We throw our overnight bags into the kids' room. The girls and Leo are getting drinks. I drop a box of groceries into the kitchen, then race into the bedroom before anyone comes back in. I dive for my backpack. Good. My fungus is still in one piece. I hid it in the side pocket. I drag it out. Oh no, it's looking pale. The white blobs are pink in places, the green looks blackish. I slide my fungus back into the side pocket. Later. Need to focus on now. I open my backpack. Yes, the tin of orange paint, brushes, rags, turpentine are all there.

Samantha has charged in and plunked Floppy on her bed. She is lying on him. That dog is getting flatter by the moment. Anna arrives with bed sheets and Leo. She is laughing at something Leo has said. 'What's so funny?'

Anna throws sheets at me. 'You are.' They land on my head. Everyone laughs.

We tuck sheets under mattresses. Samantha and Anna are already finished. I struggle with the last corner of my sheet. I hate making beds.

My bed is made. Right. I grab my backpack. 'I'll see you later.'

'Where are you going?' Nosey Samantha pipes up.

'None of your business.'

'Where are you going, Jack?' Anna flashes her dimples at me.

I've got to tell her. 'The seawall.'

'I'm coming,' Nosey says. Then everyone wants to come.

I try to persuade them that they are too tired, that Leo can show them his computer games. 'What about TV?' No luck. The more I talk, the quicker they tighten their shoe laces. 'Okay, if you come, you can't bother me. Right?' I glance through the open door at Mum and Rob. 'I've been planning this for ages.'

Samantha gets all flappy. She loves plans. 'Yes, yes.'

'I'll give you all the details when we get down there. Just let me talk Mum into letting us go out. Act casual. Hey, Mum, we're just walking to the port. We'll be back later.'

Mum crinkles her nose. 'Oh, I don't know, Jack. It can be rough near the seawall and it's getting late.'

'The sun is still shining, Mum.' I am only half-listening to her reasons as I strap on my backpack. Samantha, Anna and Leo are right behind me. 'Mum, I've been there lots of times.' I look at the others. 'And there are four of us.'

Rob has just walked in. I give him the nod. 'We're just going for a walk.'

'I know the port really well.' Leo looks at Rob.

Rob is fixing Mum with a let-them-go look. 'It'll be a chance for the kids to get to know each other.'

Mum ruffles her blonde fuzz with both hands. 'Okay, okay. But be back in time for dinner.'

Rob winks at me.

As we escape from the cottage, Anna tries to sneak a look inside my bag. 'Hey, don't touch.' Anna laughs.

'So what's in your bag, Jack?' Leo grabs it.

'Hey, Leo. Let it go.'

'Come on, what's in it?'

I give it a quick yank. 'Hands off.' Leo trips.

'Stop it, Jack,' Anna pipes in.

'Just mucking about, Anna.' Leo kicks a rock across the road.

'Oh, forget it. Let's go.' It's not far to the look-out. 'We're going down the ridge.' I point to the trail.

Anna isn't too sure about doing it. 'It looks rough.'

'Trust me. It'll be fine.'

It is steep, and the rocky trail is crumbling in places. The girls follow me, holding on to shrubs for balance. Then Anna lets out a scream. I turn around. She is doing a massive slide, her joggers are like roller blades slipping and slithering. I throw my bag of paint to the side and quickly lean against a tree for support. I hold out my hands and Anna is hurled into my arms.

Samantha is yelling, 'Anna, Anna. Are you all right?'

I shout back, 'She's okay.' I keep holding Anna until her breathing calms down. She clings on to me. I let her cling for as long as she likes.

Leo comes up behind us. 'Are you all right, Anna?'

Suddenly she lets go of me. 'I'm all right.'

We are all extra careful going down the rest of the trail. I keep checking to make sure the girls are managing. Leo is guiding Anna. Why is he holding her hand? She lets go of Leo's hand when we reach flat land. I scramble next to her. 'This way, everyone.'

It is late afternoon now, so there are only a few swimmers out in the surf. We reach the seawall. It juts out into the ocean like a spearhead. 'Looks wild.' Anna twirls her licorice curls. 'So why are we here, Jack?'

'Yeah, why?' Leo mocks.

Leo is getting on my nerves already. 'Right, I'll show you.' We walk past boulders covered in paint and graffiti. This is such great stuff. Samantha gets very excited at a dolphin drawing. There are heaps of reunion messages and 'I Luv U' hearts. Some of the illustrations are fantastic, especially one of Superman. That inspires me.

'Find a big, unpainted rock,' I order. Anna locates a medium-sized triangular boulder. I inspect. 'Good one.' I take out paint and brushes.

'What are you doing?' Anna looks nervously around.

'I know.' Leo grins.

I ignore him. 'Everyone does it. What do you want to paint?'

'Nothing.' Anna bites her bottom lip. 'It's wrong to do it. It's graffiti. We could go to gaol for that.'

'It is not graffiti.'

'Some people say it's art, others say it's not.' Leo scratches under his cap. 'No one is quite sure.'

'Well, I say it's art.' I open the tin of paint, then look at Anna. 'It is definitely not graffiti.'

'I don't think you're right, Jack.'

'It's only graffiti if it is on fences or garage doors or places it's not supposed to be. This is supposed to be here.' I stand up straight. 'I don't graffiti.'

'If you want to do this, then you ARE a graffitist.' Anna stands with her feet apart and her arms crossed. 'Once my parents' supermarket was attacked by vandals. They covered Papa's sign in black and red paint. You couldn't even read "Delicioso" or "Fruitologist". Mamma cried. I did too. We worked all day painting and fixing up the sign.'

'This is different. Are there any "Delicioso" signs? Are there any "Fruitologist" signs?'

'I'm going back.' Her nose crinkles determinedly. She looks at Samantha, then Leo. 'Are you coming?'

This is looking bad. I didn't even want them to come, but I can't let Anna storm off. I've got to think quickly. 'Wait, wait.' It is NOT graffiti. Have to really think. Idea, idea needed. I look around and see a grandfather-type person walking a dog. Got it. 'Look, what if I ask him? He'll know if we can.'

Anna squints at the old man. The dog is wagging its tail madly. It has something in its mouth. A saliva-dripping tennis ball. Samantha doesn't care. She loves dogs more than she hates saliva-dripping tennis balls. The dog looks up at her as she pats its short brown fur. 'He's gorgeous.' Gorgeous? I don't think so. The dog drops the ball and licks her hand. 'What's his name?'

The grandfather-type person smiles at Samantha. 'Wrestler.' I can see why his dog is called Wrestler. Its face is squashed nearly flat and its dribbly tongue hangs out. Its shoulders are huge, with this little body and a curly tail behind.

I squint at Anna. She is waiting.

'Excuse me,' I say. The grandfather-type person stops.

Samantha butts in. 'He's my brother.' He smiles at me. Good work, Samantha.

I give him a leading question. 'Everyone paints these rocks, don't they?'

'Yes.' He speaks slowly.

I stammer. This is the risky part. Hope he is on the side of the town that thinks the rock painting is art. 'Is it allowed?' I cross my fingers.

He thinks for a while. 'Don't know, but everyone does it. It's a tourist attraction.' He laughs. 'Except some people think it has the opposite effect.'

'So it's okay?'

He pats Wrestler. 'I enjoy looking at them.'

'My sister wants to paint a picture of a dog.'

'Like Wrestler,' Samantha pipes in. Samantha is so useful sometimes.

'That will be nice. Very nice. A picture of Wrestler? Hmmm.' He pats his dog, which dribbles on his hand. 'I'll look for it tomorrow on my evening walk.' The grandfather-type person waves as he strolls off, walking beside his squashed-face dog.

'So, Anna. You have to help Samantha paint the dog for the old man, or he'll be disappointed.'

Anna still isn't sure. Leo and Anna stand watching me while I get out the paint, prepare the boulder, wet my brushes.

Samantha isn't interested in the graffiti issue, because dogs are much more important. She is painting Wrestler with pointy ears. 'Do you think they are too pointy?' she asks. She twirls one pigtail, thinking, until Anna gives in and smoothes out the pointy bits. Then Anna writes the name 'Wrestler' under the painting.

'Great job.' I secretly keep looking around in case the grandfather-type person is wrong. Anna will never forgive me if we go to gaol. Neither will Mr and Mrs Napoli or Mum. Well, maybe Mum would forgive me because it would be an excuse for her to demonstrate outside the gaol. So she probably wouldn't mind. Rob wouldn't care.

The girls write their names. Leo paints his own name in big letters. He whispers in my ear, 'I've always wanted to do this.'

I work hard on a 'SuperJack' logo. 'Hey, look at this.' Anna starts laughing.

Samantha is laughing too. Then Leo. 'What? What?'

'That's super all right. Ha, ha.' Anna points to the S. 'If you're backwards.'

Oh, no. It IS backwards. It was because of all the decorations on the other rocks. I got confused. 'The S is meant to be that way,' I grumble as I dump the left-over paint and used brushes in the garbage bin.

'Sure.' Samantha and Anna giggle. They won't stop giggling and saying annoying things — 'Back

Jack', 'Super Dumb', 'Jumble Jack' — 'SuperJack'. It is all very unfunny.

When Leo joins in, it becomes doubly unfunny. 'Jack's Super-duper-blooper.' Leo, Samantha and Anna are falling over each other giggling.

'All right, all right.' I start walking towards the house. 'By the way, let's keep our painted rock to ourselves. Okay?' I don't think Mum and Rob would really be angry but I don't need everyone telling them about my blooper.

I have to ask them three times before they stop laughing and say, 'Okay.' They tease me all the way back to the house until I'm laughing too. It IS funny. Super dumb is what I am sometimes. We go the long way around because of Anna's near-accident down the ridge trail.

Mum and Rob are waiting for us on the front porch, drinking coffee. 'Did you have a good time?' Mum bubbles.

I stare at everyone. Don't say a word. I don't need Rob teasing me. Mum never would. 'Sure, great time.'

No one says anything, at least for now.

Anna's parents call. What a surprise. Not. Lucky Anna doesn't say anything about the rock painting, because Mr Napoli would worry about the vandals that attacked his shop and this is NOTHING like that. Anna starts laughing on the phone. 'Puss loves pizza,' she blurts out.

'Who's Puss?' Leo asks.

He doesn't know anything. Samantha goes into a long, boring description of Puss. Nanna joins in. I am over it and go and help Mum prepare lime cordial to have with dinner.

Rob arrives with take-away fish and chips. Mum complains that it's not very healthy until Rob tickles her so much she says it is okay 'this time', and we all end up laughing. We eat on the front porch, overlooking the park. Samantha brings tomato sauce to the table. You can't have good fish and chips without tomato sauce. Nanna has a battered frankfurter. That needs tomato sauce too.

Samantha starts telling Mum about the painted rocks on the seawall. I give her a kick under the table. She flashes me a grumpy look.

I watch Nanna try to eat her battered frankfurter. Oh no, the frankfurter has slipped out of the side of her mouth. Her teeth go the other way. I tap the front of my teeth with my finger. I am going to brush them twice tonight. Important things, teeth. I look at Anna. Her teeth are small and white. She flashes them as she eats a hot chip. Hey, Leo is looking at them too.

When we finish dinner, Rob just gets up. 'Jack, you're in charge tonight.'

What's that mean?

Rob leaves the table. He doesn't even pretend that he is going to do the washing up. Anna is already clearing the dishes. 'Just want to catch up with Leo for a bit. You understand.'

Leo gets up really quickly. He looks at me, smiling. He's going to tell Rob about the orange rock painting. He's going to tell Rob about how I'm super dumb. I can tell. Rob has his arm on Leo's shoulder as they walk onto the porch.

Samantha nudges me. I nudge her back. Something is wrong here. Rob always does the washing up.

Chapter 7

Jelly Snakes

Morning. Mum swirls through the cottage doing a last-minute tidy-up. She star jumps onto the porch. Of course, Samantha copies her. I ignore them and just carry the bags out to the car. You can't do anything about Mum when she is in a star jump mood. Anna is helping Nanna struggle into the back seat. I don't want to sit next to Nanna. She'll snore and tell that dumb fish story. Anna hops in beside her. Oh no, Leo is already sitting in the middle seat, next to the window. He's sneering at Mum. I can see it. I don't want to sit next to him either. Oh, the other window seat is free. 'I bags the other window,' I shout.

Samantha is standing with Floppy under her arm and her legs glued to the ground. 'Rob and Mum said I could have the window seat.' Her nose is crinkled and her beady eyes are crunched. I shove her, but she won't budge. 'No, and I'm going to tell Mum if you push me again.' I won't win this. It's turning out badly. I plunk myself next to Leo. Samantha jumps in after me and shuts the door. She pokes out her tongue. 'I've got the window seat.'

'Me too.' Leo smiles. No, I mean, smirks. I elbow him in the side. 'Hey, that hurts.'

'Sorry, Leo. It's a bit squashed in the middle seat.'

Rob revs the car. I look out past Samantha's head through the window. The sky is blue, the sun shining. Oh, who cares about dumb window seats and dumb Leo sticking like glue? Not me. Rob zooms off, heading north. Yes, north. Beaches, fun parks. I nudge Samantha and stick my thumbs up. 'Goodbye house,' I shout.

Samantha points Floppy's paws out to sea. 'Goodbye look-out.'

'Goodbye ocean,' Mum sings.

'Goodbye teeth,' Nanna gurgles.

Suddenly, there is dead silence. Everyone turns to stare at Nanna except Rob, who is driving. Mum's hands bounce around like jumping beans. Everyone knows. We HAVE to go back. Nanna without teeth is a BIG problem. She would only be able to eat porridge and yoghurt. Rob groans, then slows down, ready to turn, when Nanna announces proudly, 'Just joking.'

Everyone laughs with relief. 'You're hilarious, Nanna.' Samantha's pudgy hand reaches over to the back seat and Nanna's wobbly hands wiggle back at her. I think I get my great humour from Nanna.

I squint at the seawall. I don't say goodbye to the seawall because of Anna. She is a bit sensitive about our rock painting. I can just make out our orange rock.

Leo notices me squinting at the boulders. 'Backwards Jack.'

'Oh, shut up, Leo,' I whisper under my breath. I wonder if he told Rob about it.

We turn out of town. As we hit the main road, Rob says that there will be no detours. No detours? Rob must be joking. I have to see the Big Bull at Wauchope and I really want to see the Big Banana at Coffs Harbour. 'Hey, Rob.'

'It's a nine-hour drive to the Gold Coast. No tourist stops, kids.'

'But there is lots to see on the way, Rob.'

'Look out of the window.'

As if I can, jammed between Samantha, Floppy and Leo. 'I haven't got the window seat.'

Rob doesn't even listen. 'At Coffs Harbour there's the Big Banana. We drive right past it.'

Nanna sparks up. 'A banana smoothie. Mmmm. We should stop there.' Nanna is right. I wait, staring at the back of Rob's golf ball head.

'Maybe we'll stop on the way back.'

That means NO. Rob won't stop on the way there or the way back. I start to argue, but Mum turns around with that look. It is her new support-Rob tactic AND right in front of Leo. 'No, Jack.'

Leo smiles. I'll wipe that smile off his face one day. This is all so unfair. 'Bananas,' I mutter under my breath as Rob zooms between forests of scribbly gum trees and along divided highways. I twist away from Leo. My head is thumping. The road cuts through mountains like a bread knife, or is it my head? Finally banana plantations appear, in the valleys, along the sides of hills, right to the peak. Thousands of trees with leafy green palms and fat yellow bananas hanging from them in pods. I'll give it one last try. 'Rob, can I . . .'

'Sorry, Jack. Another time. I promise.' Rob turns his head to look at me for a second.

'NO BIG BANANA.' Leo elbows me.

I grunt at him, 'NO BIG BULL,' then whisper in his ear, 'you bull-poo.' Leo gives me a mucky look. 'Bull-poo,' I whisper again, before I flick Rob's hair. 'NO BIG GOLF HEAD either.'

Anna laughs. Rob rubs his prickly head. Mum gives it a pat too.

'NO BIG SHEEP,' Samantha bleats. 'Baa-baa.'

'NO BIG NOISE,' I bleat back at Samantha before I tell her to shut up. But she doesn't shut up. She keeps baa-ing, baa-ing until Nanna pipes in.

Nanna is holding an empty lunch bag. 'NO BIG COOKIE.'

Mum joins in next. 'NO BIG FEAST.'

Then it starts seriously. Total nuttiness takes over the car like a virus. 'NO BIG ROCK' . . . 'NO BIG KOALA' . . . 'NO BIG MANGO' . . . 'NO BIG . . .'

As we drive past the Big Banana, I yell out, 'NO BIG IDIOTS.'

There is this dead silence for two seconds, before everyone is yelling, 'NO BIG NUTS, NO BIG BRAINS, NO BIG . . .'

I groan. 'Put on the radio, Mum. Pleassssse.'

'What, darling?' Mum splutters.

Darling? I give up. 'Radio,' I shout.

'Oh, all right.' It takes a while for the laughing to stop and Mum's music to hum through the car. There are no more BIG anythings mentioned and Samantha starts begging Mum to change the station. Mum doesn't.

Luckily Rob turns into a roadside service centre. 'Rest stop, kids.' Every two hours Rob pulls over. He says that when you're driving you don't notice how tired you get. 'Drivers fall asleep at the wheel.' I reckon that Rob is an advertisement for the road safety slogan, 'Stop, Revive, Survive'.

It is great stretching my legs, especially since I have been stuck between two blobs. Samantha blob and Leo blob. Toilet stop. Good, at least it won't be a bush can under a goanna attack. Imagine having two penises. Goanna-power. I might do some research on that when I get home. Interesting. I wonder how my fungus is. Has it turned into penicillin or something incredible?

My stomach rumbles.

'Hamburgers and milkshakes for everyone?'

'Rob, Rob can I have a double burger with cheese and bacon?'

'Me too,' Leo copies, which is really annoying.

Rob rubs my head, then puts one hand on Leo's shoulder. 'You kids must be starving.'

'Yes, yes, yes.' Leo and I race towards the counter.

Rob smiles. 'Good to see you boys getting along.'

I don't know about that. I glance at Leo, then Rob. Rob really, truly, desperately wants me to get on with Leo. I guess I have to try but it's a BIG ask. Hey, is that funny? NO BIG ASK. I can add that to the NO BIG list.

Nanna, Mum and Rob sit together. The kids sit at another table. I gulp down the last bite of hamburger.

'Everyone finished?'

I look at Samantha and Anna. 'Do you want to trick Nanna?'

'It's not a mean trick, is it?' Samantha slurps the last of her lemonade.

'No, don't be stupid. Nanna will think it's funny.'

'I don't know.' Anna's dimples look like question marks. She isn't sure.

'Nanna likes a joke. You know that.'

'What are you planning?' Leo leans forward to listen as I whisper the great trick. 'But I can't be in it,' Leo complains.

'Next time, Leo.' It's family stuff. 'We'll do it when Nanna gets into the car. Okay?'

The 'Stop, Revive, Survive' pit stop is over. Rob is looking at his watch. Nanna is shuffling towards us. I elbow Samantha, then Anna. 'Ready?' I whisper under my breath.

'Ready.' Anna.

'Ready.' Samantha.

From the corner of my eye, I see Leo slumping against the car.

'FLASH,' I shout. 'NOW.'

We all drop our shorts and dive for our toes. Our bums are in the air, our underpants are flashing, glowing. Purple.

Nanna chuckles and clucks. She gets so excited that she flashes her own underpants back at us. Yes, they are purple too. We end up in a howling heap. We can't believe it. Nanna is wearing her purple underpants too. She must have a secret supply of them.

Mum turns around to see. Her face drops disappointedly. 'I wish I was wearing mine.'

Rob rubs his chin, trying to hide a smile.

'I'll buy you a pair of purple underpants too, Leo.' Nanna puffs up with satisfaction at her clever bargain hunting.

'That'd be really great.' Leo mutters under his breath, 'Not.' He doesn't get it. Purple underpants. It's something big that Nanna wants to buy him a pair. Luckily Nanna doesn't see. That is mainly because she's talking to Rob, who is excited that Nanna wants to buy Leo purple underpants. Rob gets it. I think sawdust is coming out of Rob's ears. Ha, ha.

Oh, the sawdust has stopped. Rob is in the driver's seat. 'Get comfortable, everyone. It's a long drive to get there.'

Mum says that Samantha HAS to swap seats with me. Samantha kicks me. 'Stop pressing against me, Jack.'

'So now you know what it's like.'

She flaps Floppy's paw in my face. I squash Floppy's nose. What else could I do? Samantha aims Floppy's bum at me. Suddenly Mum's hand grabs Floppy. 'No teasing.' Mum only gives Floppy back to Samantha when we both promise to stop arguing. I stare out of the window now that I have the window seat AT LAST. We drive and drive. Then we drive some more. It is getting so boring. I kick Samantha. She whines back at me. Mum turns around. 'Stop it, Jack.' She passes out a packet of jelly snakes. Everyone takes a snake. Anna and Samantha have a stretching game. How long can they stretch a red jelly snake? They have to be careful. They measure it. It's twenty-four centimetres. Wow. Snap. Ha, ha. Samantha eats her half of the snake. Anna throws her half to me. I eat it. Then we have a snake stretching competition.

Nanna has a go. Her knobbly hands make it hard to pull. She loses, but I give her a whole snake. She really wants a red snake. Bits stick between her teeth. When will we be there? When? When? Oh no, Nanna takes out her teeth to get to the jelly bits. I am going to be sick.

Leo laughs at her. He presses back on the car seat, whispering to me behind Samantha's back, 'Toothless old bat.'

Pushing Samantha aside with one hand, I take a swing at Leo. 'Shut up.'

Leo yells out, 'I didn't do anything. Stop it. Why are you hitting me?'

He knows why. He does. I stick my finger up at him as he nurses his arm. He is putting on this over-the-top show, moaning and gulping as loudly as he can.

Mum and Rob don't even ask what happened. They just shout at me. 'Why did you do that, Jack?'

What am I supposed to say?

'Are you all right, Leo?' Mum apologises. All right? What does that mean? Mum and Rob are horrible, lecturing me on being nice to poor little Leo. Yeah, sure. Leo called Nanna a terrible name. My nanna. Mum and Rob wouldn't believe me even if I told them. And Nanna can never know. 'I'm really disappointed in you, Jack,' Mum says quietly. Well, I'm disappointed in Mum.

Rob turns to stare at me. It's only for a few seconds, but there is this awful look in his eyes. He hates me. My head is exploding. What can I say? Nothing. Anna shakes her head at me. Everyone is against me. I turn away and press my face against the window. Leo stops whingeing eventually. Mum puts on Samantha's CD and the car whizzes ahead.

'Where are the rest of the jelly snakes?' Samantha suddenly looks around.

There is a search. I don't even try to look. Everything has been so unfair. How I am supposed to like Leo? And Rob hates me. This choking feeling makes me gasp for air.

'The packet must have fallen under the seat.' Nanna smiles. 'I'll buy you all some more jelly snakes later.' She is so kind. I give Leo a dirty look.

'Don't worry about the jelly snakes or anything else.' Mum turns around and touches my hand. 'We're all going to have a good time together.'

I'm not so sure.

Hours, hours, hours. The sun blares into the car. Nanna is the first to nod off, then Anna. There is a duet going on in the back — Nanna and Anna snoring. Leo is leaning against the other window. Good, he can stay there. Samantha has collapsed into Floppy's fur. I feel my eyelids getting heavier. It's the sun, the glare . . . zzzzzzzzzzzzz.

I doze and wake, doze and wake. Leo's face sticks into my head like fungus. Oh, my fungus. It likes the sun. It should be growing a lot. Mum's and Rob's talk sifts in and out of my head. 'World peace . . .' Mum's favourite topic. 'Why do you think Jack hit Leo?' 'Maybe he's jealous.' 'They're just kids. It's too early, but they'll work it out. They just have to get used to each other.' I am never going to get used to Leo. I just want Mum and Rob. Rob is our . . . I try to speak, but the sun . . . I wonder if the bottle is big enough for my fungus. Hope the fluids aren't oozing out. Yawn. It likes the heat . . . heat . . . yawn . . . zzzzzzzzzzzzzzz.

Someone is shaking me. 'What? What?' Fungus attack. It is HUGE, white, slimy, stinky. I start hitting the fungal growths. 'Fungus,' I moan.

'Jack, stop it. I'm not fungus.' Blonde frizz is hitting my face. 'Jack, Jack. It's Mum. Wake up. We're here, darling. The Gold Coast. We're here.'

I'm confused. Where am I? 'Darling? Don't call me darling.'

Mum is smiling at me. I look around blearily. Ah, I am still in the car. Rob's head peers over the front seat. What a big golf-ball head. Ha, ha. Oh, I remember. He hates me. There's Nanna. Anna is running her fingers through her dark hair. She is beautiful. No, I don't mean that. I shake my head. 'Wake up, Jack.' I blink hard twice, rub my face with both hands.

We're here.

Chapter 8

Star Jumps and Sun Hats

Mum unloads Nanna from the car. It's a big job, since her leg has fallen asleep. I don't want to know. I am still getting over the fungus attack. We pile out of the other car door. The sky is red. There is a cool breeze. Palm trees are waving in the wind.

'Look, Jack.' Mum points to the holiday apartment. It's painted tropical yellow with a wide balcony AND it is right opposite the beach just like Mum promised. It looks fantastic. 'You kids had better shake the sleep out of your heads before we unpack. Jump up and down. It'll get your blood circulating.' Mum takes two deep breaths, then starts doing star jumps. Everything is shaking on her. Samantha star jumps too. Then Anna starts jumping. It must be a girl disease. I am out of here.

Rob is leaning on the back of the four-wheel drive, watching the surf. He calls out to me. 'Over here Jack.' I'm not so sure. He keeps waving at me to come.

'All right, all right.'

'Leo, over here too.' We lean next to Rob on the car. 'This morning is over. Okay? We're going to have a great time. Okay?' Rob puts his arm on Leo's shoulder, then mine. He repeats himself. 'Okay?'

I nod. So does Leo.

'Surf looks good, boys.'

Rob is right. Surf. Beach. There is sand for as far as you can see — both ways. Waves are rolling in like sausage dogs. My humour is returning. Dog jokes. I must be feeling okay. 'Sausage dogs,' I call out to Samantha, pointing to the waves.

'What?' she calls back.

'Come on. Stop mucking around. Beach.' I chase the girls until they are squealing little piggies. 'Oink, oink.' I laugh as I tackle them onto the sand.

'I give up,' they both squeal together. I let them get up, then chase them back to Mum.

Rob and Leo are still leaning against the four-wheel drive, talking. I wonder what they're talking about.

The apartment is the best. It has a huge window in the lounge room that overlooks the beach. All the floors are tiled in a creamy flecked tile, which means that we don't have to worry about bringing sand inside or spilling drinks. It is a four-bedroom apartment. There is a race for rooms. The girls get the bedroom with a balcony and two single beds. In the boys' room, there is a bunk bed and no balcony. Leo throws his gear onto the bottom bunk. 'I've got this one.' He smiles. I shrug.

We run in and out unpacking when I suddenly just have to stop. Samantha crashes into my back. It is Rob. He is holding a thermometer. I can't believe it. Rob smiles as he hangs it on the wall. 'We have to know how hot it gets up here.'

Samantha and I burst out laughing.

'Not that funny.' Rob winks at us.

Leo nudges me. 'What are you laughing at?'

'Don't worry. It's just Rob. Inside joke.'

Leo's face creases into a frown. What is wrong with him? It's just a private joke.

Nanna is lucky. There's a comfortable armchair next to the window. Nanna knows straightaway that that chair is hers. As she sits down in it, she grins. 'I can look at you all from here.' The chair is right opposite the TV as well. These days Nanna watches a lot of TV with the volume up HIGH. She used to play the violin in the Senior Citizens' Bush Band, but that was before her hearing went. She misses that. She misses Grandad too.

Mum announces that she is too tired to cook, even though there is a super-modern kitchen in the apartment. Better than the one at home Nanna is too tired to go out, as well. Rob, Leo and I are given the job of buying dinner Barbecue chicken with herb stuffing, fresh bread, coleslaw and potato salad. It is a feast. Nanna loves the potato salad. It doesn't stick in her teeth.

Anna phones her parents to say she has arrived safely. She wasn't eaten by a goanna or run over by a cane toad. Mr Napoli should be happy about all that.

Leo rings his mother too. He presses his shoulder against the wall and turns away from us. I listen for a bit. Gee, his mother seems to want to know everything about us, especially about Rob and Mum. 'No, they don't fight,' he mutters. 'She's okay. But you're my mum, okay?'

First day on the Gold Coast. I am up early. Breakfast.
Samantha is setting the table. Anna is grilling bacon
and toasting bread. Leo is plugged into his laptop
computer. I watched him play it last night for a
while. He said that I could have a go but he never let
me. He let Anna have a turn but only for a few
minutes. In the end, we just walked away. I am
squeezing enough juice for everyone on Rob's super
orange squisher. We had to bring it, otherwise Rob
would have had serious orange squisher withdrawal
symptoms. I think that means frothing at the mouth
or dribbling like a tap. Ha, ha.

'Surprise,' we all shout when Mum and Rob come
out of their bedroom. 'Breakfast made just for you,'
I add.

'How lovely.' Mum kisses Samantha. Mum doesn't
realise that we have ulterior motives. We need Mum
and Rob relaxed when we hit them with our plans
for the Gold Coast.

We don't wait for Nanna because she usually
sleeps in. Rob is drinking his orange juice. 'Where's
Leo?' he asks.

I start telling Mum and Rob about the BIG plans,
when Rob just heads for Leo. 'Hey, Rob,' I call out,
but he ignores me. We wait ages for him to come
back. At last Leo is following Rob to the kitchen. He
has obviously finished his computer game. Okay.

Leo is sitting down now. Rob is sitting too. Oh, Rob is drinking the terrific orange juice we made. A good moment. I use my brains and start talking about Mum's and Rob's excellent choices — the great beaches, the fantastic weather, the tropical apartment. Soften them up.

Mum laughs. 'What do you want?'

Mum wrecks everything. Oh well, I might as well launch into it. 'Can we go to see the dolphins today?' I move my hands into the shape of a diving dolphin. That should impress Rob and Mum.

'And what about water slides?' Samantha asks.

Anna pokes me. 'Oh yes, and a theme park, and . . .'

'Hold on, hold on.' Rob is spluttering his juice.

'Are you okay, Rob?' Don't want our driver to choke. Samantha jumps up to rub his back. She is a crawler, but in this situation it's a good thing.

'I can see why you kids made such a great breakfast.' Mum smiles. 'Bribery?'

'No way, Mum.' I look innocently at her. Anyway, Mum is the queen of bribery. She is always bribing us with ice creams and bubble gum to tidy our rooms and do our homework. It works, sometimes.

Rob is shaking his head. 'Today we'll get our bearings. Let you kids really get to know each other, drive around the beaches, maybe swim. A relaxing day. Your mum and I need to unwind.'

'But, but . . .'

'Tomorrow, the dolphins, then we'll see.'

I start to argue, then realise Rob is not in a reasonable mood. Then I think. Hey, beaches today, dolphins tomorrow. Theme park for sure, the day after.

'Get ready. We're going for a drive now, kids.'

I grab the last piece of bacon. Anna made it crunchy. Just the way I like it. 'Coming, Samantha? Anna?' Rob squints at me. I know what he wants. I yell, 'Coming, Leo?'

'In a minute,' Leo answers with his mouth full of mashed toast.

'The dishes . . .' Mum's voice disappears as I slam my bedroom door. I couldn't wash the dishes up while Mum and Rob were still eating. Mum knows that.

I check out my jar of fungus, which I put under the bed. Wow, it's looking excellent. The white marshmallow growths are mutating into lumps and the green parts are darker. I crawl under the bottom bunk and stick it back underneath. Hey, what's that? There is a crackly sound. What is it? Something is stuck in the slats of Leo's bunk. I drag it out. It's the left-over packet of jelly snakes we were looking for in the car. Why would he take it? Who'd want to eat jelly snakes by themselves? That's no fun. I shake my head. Leo is a thief for sure. I stuff the packet of jelly snakes under my blanket on the top bunk for now.

We are ready to go. Mum leaves a note for Nanna saying we'll be back by lunch time. I race towards the car. Leo calls out, 'Dad, can I sit in the front seat?'

Dad? I turn around and stare at Leo and Rob. Tingles crawl down my neck. Dad? But Leo doesn't even really know Rob. Rob lives with us. Hey, Leo is climbing into the front seat. That's Mum's spot. No one else is allowed to sit there, except on special occasions.

'Leo and Rob need to talk about a lot of things,' Mum explains as she gets into the back.

'They're always talking,' I mumble. It's just a crummy excuse that Leo has made up to get into the front seat.

Mum's daffodil scarf flutters behind her as she gets into the car.

'That's so pretty.' Samantha wiggles her fingers between the folds.

Mum has bubble gum balls in her pocket. (Bribery.) She gives us two each, then she taps Leo's shoulder. 'Do you want some bubble gum, Leo?' He sticks his hand out and Mum gives him only ONE bubble gum ball. Good, he deserves that. He doesn't even say thank you to Mum. He shouldn't get even one gum ball.

Rob pulls into Kirra Beach so we can all watch the surfboard riders. 'It has some of the best waves in the world.' Rob watches the waves for ages. Then I notice two surfie girls with long blonde hair. I whistle.

Anna goes nuts. 'Sexist,' she explodes with her cannonball eyes.

I could be in trouble here. 'It's only a joke, Anna. You like my jokes.'

'Not this one.'

I am going to say sorry when Leo butts in. 'Some jokes aren't funny.'

'That's right.' Anna crosses her arms.

I want to kick Leo in the shins, except I can't reach him. What's he up to?

'Jack is just being dumb, Anna.' Samantha shrugs. 'He's told me that there's no one as pretty as you.'

I feel my head thumping. How could Samantha say that? Then I notice Anna trying not to smile. 'This time I'll forget your grossness, Jack. Only this time.' She pretends to be angry.

Saved by the Samantha. Phew.

Coolangatta is definitely a holiday town — surf shops, cafés, heaps of people. The Coolangatta Surf Life Saving Club is right in the middle of the beach. 'There's a pie shop.' Samantha spies it straightaway. She has excellent eyes when she is looking for meat pies or cream buns.

'We'll get some later for lunch.' Mum kisses Samantha.

Rob parks near the escarpment on the other side of Coolangatta. We start climbing to the top. It's steep and I have to pull Samantha up behind me. Leo runs ahead of us. 'I'll get there first.'

I raise my eyebrows. Who cares? 'Good,' I call after him. I have to help Samantha, anyway.

'Lucky we didn't bring Nanna.' Samantha gasps. 'She'd have to stay in the car, and it's too hot in the back seat today.'

Nanna. Mum and Rob keep having secret talks about her. Sometimes I catch a bit of their conversations. '. . . can't live by herself any more.' 'What if she falls and no one finds her for days?'

I drag Samantha up the final peak. Samantha's ears are red. Really red like hot chilli. 'Your ears.' I point to them. 'Ha. Ha. Are you going to explode?' That is hilarious. 'Ha, ha. Exploding Samantha.'

'Stop it, Jack. I'm boiling.'

But I don't stop it. Fun is fun. 'Red ears. You're an exploding pixie. What is short and red all over? A sunburnt pixie reading the newspaper. Do you get it? Red and read.' Samantha isn't laughing. 'Red is the colour of the pixie and read is what you do when you have a newspaper.' Samantha just ignores me.

Anna wanders up to us. 'It's beautiful here, isn't it?' I stop teasing Samantha. I see Leo further up the escarpment. Anna notices him too. 'He's nice, Jack, isn't he?'

Is Anna kidding? I want to tell her about what he said about Nanna, and now there are the jelly

94

snakes. But I have second thoughts. Leo isn't nice to Mum either. He's always trying to get Rob to himself.

Anna is bending over the railing with her hair blowing in the wind. I move next to her. It's great with just Anna, Samantha and me here. We can see beaches stretching right up to the Gold Coast with its skyscrapers. They look like matchboxes on the horizon.

Racing back down the hill is fast and furious. I'm first to reach the bottom. Leo is second. 'I fell,' he said.

'You didn't fall.' Samantha pants.

'I did,' Leo complains, as he gets into the front seat AGAIN.

We clamber into the car, stop at the pie shop, have another quick look at Kirra Beach. Wish Rob had let us bring our surfboard from Sydney, but he said there was no room. Hope Nanna is awake when we get back to the apartment.

We're back. I jump over the balcony and open the doors. Nanna waves at me. Everyone races inside to get their swimmers and towels. 'We're going to the beach, Nanna. Come on.'

'Oh good. I'll just be a minute, Jack.' It takes her ages to get her orthopaedic shoes on.

'Ready now, Nanna?'

'Nearly.' Come on. She has to find her bag and her walking stick.

Nearly out of the door. Great. Oh, no.

'I forgot to take my medicine.' I moan. Nanna will be getting ready forever. She waddles back to the kitchen bench. She takes her medicine, then has a cookie.

We pile into the car. Rob puts on the yellow cap Nanna bought him.

'Let's go. Beach, beach, beach,' we yell.

It is boiling hot and we wind down the windows. The wind blasting through is great. Anna's hair tangles into curls and Samantha's ponytail bobs. (She gets sick of pigtails sometimes.) 'Can you close the windows please, children?'

'It's hot, Nanna.'

But she just puts her hands in front of her face. 'It's too blowy.'

Mum makes us close the windows. 'That's fine,' Leo says. What a crawler. Rob has turned on the air conditioning. It's all right for Leo, since he's in the front seat where the cold air blasts into his face. It will take ages for the air to get into the back seats. Nanna wants us to suffocate. Air, air. It's so dumb. We can never ever have the car windows rolled down, all because of her hair. Nanna and her stupid hair. It's hard, like a rock. The wind won't move her hair. Not even a hurricane will. It is solid.

How long is the air conditioning going to take to get to the back? Air, air. I look at Nanna and her hard head. She is nearly unconscious from the heat.

But no, as long as her hair is stuck together she's happy.

'Are we nearly there, Rob?' I am hot and sticky.

Samantha sees the name Mermaid Beach. 'Please can we go there, Rob? I think it has a lovely name.' That is the stupidest reason I ever heard for going to a beach, but Rob is a sucker for Samantha. I bet if I asked him, he wouldn't. Who cares? We have to stop or die. Rob wheels into a car spot. I pour myself out of the back seat into a pool of sweat.

Beach umbrella, fold-up chairs, pies from Samantha's pie shop. They are a bit cold, but still delicious. Mermaid Beach looks good, even with that pathetic name. We finish lunch quickly, then race for the water. It's warm. We jump under waves, over waves. Samantha dives between my legs. I stand on my hands in the water. Then I jump up and carry Anna on my shoulders. 'Hey Leo, you carry Samantha. We can have a game. See who knocks over the other first.' Samantha scrambles onto Leo's shoulders. Anna climbs onto mine. Then it's on. We charge and scream. The girls wrestle until Anna crashes into the sea.

'Are you okay, Anna?' Leo calls out, but Anna has already surfaced and is climbing back onto my shoulders.

'You're not bad at this Leo, but watch out.' I charge him.

Samantha crashes in the water, then Anna, then I lose it. Crash. Anna and I look like drowned octopuses. (I don't dare even mention the FISH word.) I spurt a mouthful of sea water into the air, and we end up in a mouth spurting competition. Samantha's spurt is the highest until she swallows, choking on salt water. 'Need a drink,' she splutters.

Me too. 'Drinks, drinks.'

We splatter and splash out of the water. When we reach Mum, I do a doggy shake and drips fly everywhere. Mum wags her hand at us. Her face is red. 'Sorry.' I must have splashed Mum. Nanna's face is red too. Rob folds his newspaper in half.

Mum tells us to take the lemonade. 'It's hot today.' She ties on her yellow sun hat. One of Nanna's famous special buys. 'Samantha, put on your sun hat.' She ties the ribbon under Samantha's chin.

Nanna plops her yellow sun hat on carefully because she doesn't want to wreck her hard head. When Anna puts hers on, Nanna's face creases into a huge crinkly smile. 'Everyone looks beautiful in their sun hats.'

'From Susie's Splendid Discount Store.' Samantha giggles. We stare at each other for a second. Then Samantha points to Rob's yellow cap and we burst out laughing.

I rub my head. I put on my yellow cap. 'We're the yellow family. Looks like we have growths on our heads.' My fungus comes straight into my mind. It's going to be a monster by the end of this holiday. My secret.

Everyone is looking the other way when Leo kicks sand in front of him. It hits Samantha's back. 'Hey, watch out, Leo,' I rumble at him as I stand in front of Samantha.

'Sorry, Samantha. Accident.' Leo is lying. 'Haven't got a hat,' he announces.

Rob looks up, then throws Leo his yellow hat. Why did Rob do that? Leo can live without a hat.

We drink lemonade under our beach umbrella listening to the waves crashing onto the sand. 'The beach. The sun. Aren't we lucky to live in Australia?' Mum's eyes are soft like melting butter. She blinks, and a little butter seems to drip out of the corner of her eyes.

'You're right.' Rob's face is getting sunburnt. No hat.

Mum is reading the newspaper. 'I'm sick of bullies. People who want to force you to think the way they do.' She looks at us. Oh, this must be one of Mum's world peace talks. Rob takes the newspaper and flashes the headlines and photos of destroyed buildings and shell-shocked people.

I dig my big toe into the sand. I have thought about this for a while. I just know there will always be fighting somewhere, somehow. There will always be bullies and George Hamels, with dumb idiots who follow them. 'We won't let them, Mum.'

'No, we won't let them.' Mum holds up the newspaper. 'If everyone does just something small to stop it, then it mightn't happen.' She pushes back the blonde fuzz escaping from her sun hat. 'There is a march in Sydney next week. "Say NO to Terrorism."' She looks at each of us, then asks, 'Can we walk in that march together?'

Samantha nods so hard that her sun hat flops to over her eyes. 'Yes. Yes, Mum.' Anna nods. Rob nods. Even Nanna says that she will march, and she can't walk.

'Dad, I don't live in Sydney. I can't go.'

Dad. It feels weird when Leo calls Rob that. Anyway, it is Mum's idea. Leo should talk to Mum.

'Why don't you stay with us for that weekend?' Rob looks at me. 'We can put a mattress on the floor in Jack's bedroom.'

What? My room? There is no space. My scientific experiments can't be moved. Leo won't fit. I can't believe Rob just gave my room, or the floor, to Leo.

'That would be good, Dad.'

But it's MY bedroom. Rob is smiling. This feels awful. 'It's okay with you, Jack, isn't it?'

'Sure.' What else can I say? Maybe it won't happen. That makes me feel a bit better.

We pack up our gear. Leo gets into the front seat. Mum sees a fruit market on the way back from Mermaid Beach. Tropical Queensland has the best fruit. Drippy mangoes, sweet pineapples, fat bananas, bumpy-lumpy custard apples that are the best. Mum buys some spiky red rambutans as well. She also buys oranges of course, for Rob.

'Don't bring sand inside.' Mum swirls into the apartment, making the daisies on her skirt look like they're flying. I am carrying a heavy bag of fruit. Samantha is biting into a banana. Oh, that reminds me. I must check my fungus.

Mum cuts up a plate of fruit for us and we head towards the girls' room. It is a private feast. 'Coming, Leo?' Anna smiles at him.

'Don't you want to play your computer games, Leo?' The ones you haven't let Samantha or Anna or me try? I don't even care about playing the games. I care that Leo can't seem to share them.

'Later, Jack.'

What an unexpected answer. He never misses out on anything he wants. I shake my head.

Anna throws a rug on the floor in the girls' bedroom, then lays out the tropical feast in the middle of it. I slump onto the rug. Samantha grabs Floppy and lies on him. By the end of this holiday, he's going to be flatter for sure. I take a rambutan and throw it to Samantha. She loves the sweet white fruit inside even more than I do.

'Can't wait to see the dolphins tomorrow.' Samantha dribbles her rambutan over Floppy. Poor dog. Now he's flat, and sticky too.

'I'm glad we're walking against terrorism. Your Mum is amazing.' Anna's chocolate drop eyes are serious. 'It's great that we'll be walking together.'

Leo leans on his elbows. He glances at Anna, then me. 'Thanks for letting me stay in your room, Jack.'

'I'm sure Jack doesn't mind.' Anna bites into a piece of banana.

'It's okay.' Sort of.

Chapter 9

Nanna's Underpants Save the Day

I sleep like a log. Sun blares through the curtains, which were left half-open last night. It's morning, bright and early. I jump out of bed. Leo is asleep. I head for the girls' room. 'Hey Samantha, get up.'

Grumble. 'Get lost, Jack.' She squeals when I pull off her blanket, but I'll torture her later. Don't want to wake up Anna.

There is a bowl of frangipanis on the lounge room table. Mum must be up already. Yep, I'm right. Sandwiches are laid out and drinks are lined up on the kitchen bench. Mum dances into the room wearing her sunflower blouse and matching sunflower skirt. 'We're going to have a great day, Jack.' She finishes packing the sandwiches.

I check out Rob's thermometer in the kitchen. Thirty-three degrees already. It's going to be a hot one.

'Hi, Nanna.' She is eating her breakfast of porridge. She has made a special effort to get up early so that we won't be late for the dolphins. I check out the beach through the full-size lounge room window. Surfers are waxing their boards on the beach. Lifesavers are watching from their tower for undertows and swimmers caught in rips. I gulp. I was caught once in a rip.

'Nanna, do you want some orange juice?' She nods and I squeeze. I'll make some for everyone.

I hate remembering that rip. Tried to swim across it. That's like swimming against cement. In the end I let the rip take me. Looked like I was heading for Antarctica, except the lifesaver didn't let me get to Antarctica. My life flashed in front of my eyes. How would Mum cope without me? Samantha too. The lifesaver reminded me of Rob. 'Are you all right, son?' the lifesaver had asked. I felt like crying when he called me that. I didn't cry, of course. I've never told Mum about it.

I drink juice and eat porridge with Nanna. I blink twice when Anna enters the room. She is wearing hot pink board shorts and a white T-shirt with 'Angel' written on it in silver. She does a pirouette like a ballerina. There are silver wings on the back. 'How do I look?'

'Gorgeous,' Samantha yawns, straggling after her. She is so right. Rob sticks his thumb up at me.

Anna sits next to me and I start teasing her about her wings. 'You're really a bird now. A chirpy bird.'

'Hilarious, Jack.'

Leo rumbles in, scratching his neck. Then he stops. He just stands there like a stuffed emu staring at Anna.

'Hey, haven't you seen wings before, Leo?'

'Not ones like those. You look terrific, Anna.'

She blushes. 'Thank you, Leo.'

Oh, I meant to say that. Now I can't. Anna does look terrific.

'Dolphins, dolphins,' Mum hums around the table.

'I love them,' Samantha cheeps. She holds up her dolphin necklace for Rob to see. Firstly, everyone knows she loves dolphins and secondly, Rob bought her that dolphin necklace. 'I love this. I really do.' She hugs Rob. She'll do anything for attention.

I have to get out of here before my orange juice regurgitates. I grab my camera and scramble through the front door. 'Just going to take a few pictures.' Outside. Fresh air. Good. What is that tweeting? I look around. There's a lot of noise. Well, squawking. What is it? I see them. Oh wow. There have to be at least twenty in that eucalyptus tree. I leave my camera on the front step and walk carefully towards them. Hey, they're not scared. A couple look up at me. These rosellas are used to visitors for sure. I dig into my pocket. I am in luck. A half-eaten left-over cookie is still there. It's a bit crunched up and crumbly, but they like it that way. I hold out my hand. Two bright red and green rosellas land, pecking at the crumbs. Their parrot beaks tickle, but I don't move. Oh no, one has landed on my head.

'Where are you, Jack?' Samantha runs outside looking for me.

'Here, here.' I slide the words out of the side of my mouth.

Samantha sees me. 'Wow.'

'Shush . . . camera.'

Samantha is smart. She tiptoes towards my camera, so as not to frighten the birds away. Click, click, click. They will be great photos.

As she clicks I whisper, 'Tell everyone to come out, with cookies.'

The next thing I know Mum is standing beside me with a rosella pecking cookies from her hands. One swoops at Rob's spiky head. Probably thinks there are seeds there! Another one lands on Leo's shoulder, hopping towards the cookies. There is a bright red and green rosella on Anna's silver wing. Samantha is still clicking. Nanna watches from the lounge room window. She waves at us. She's happy that they like her cookies.

Cookies are finished and the birds hop back into their tree. That was fantastic. Oh no, I look at Rob's head. There is a big sticky white plop there. Ha, ha. Samantha runs in to get a tissue for Rob's head.

'Plop-head, Plop-head,' I shout. Rob chases me around the frangipani tree and tackles me onto the lawn until we're both puffing and laughing. Leo chases after us. Rob has me in a pretend head lock. 'Sorry Rob . . . sorry . . .' I gasp. 'You're not a plop-head.' I can't stop laughing.

Rob lets go, then suddenly Leo tackles me. We wrestle for a bit. He tries to kick me in the stomach but misses. I am too quick and grab his leg. When I get him down, I jump away. Rob thinks it's a game. I'm not so sure.

As Leo struggles up, something falls out of his shorts. 'Hey. What's that?'

'Nothing.' He stuffs an old silver lighter into his pocket as he scrambles next to Rob.

I'll check that lighter out some time, but not now. We're going to see dolphins today and I'm not interested in Leo and the stupid things he does. We race to get our swimming gear and lunches. I put some new film into my camera. Nanna tries to leave her walking stick behind, but we all shout at her, 'Walking stick, Nanna.'

'I hear you, I hear you.' Nanna is cunning like that.

Samantha picks pink frangipanis from the frangipani tree. They smell like honey. Mum and the girls put a flower behind their ear. Nanna doesn't because of her hard head. Samantha puts one behind Rob's ear just as the mobile phone rings. Rob leans against his four-wheel drive with a frangipani on his head and a phone next to his ear. Wonder what his boss would say. He'd never live it down. Rob and a flower. Ha, ha. I'll save that for future blackmail purposes.

'Special problem. Ummm . . . Leaks oil . . . 1980 Toyota Corona . . . Modification . . . Drive transmission . . . He'll need to take it to the workshop.' Rob gives excellent technical advice. He's promised that he'll take me to his work one day. I can't wait to go. He finishes the call. 'Let's move out. Get into the back today, Leo,' he says.

'But Dad . . .'

I'm getting half-used to hearing Leo call Rob 'Dad'. But somehow, I don't like it that much.

Rob shakes his head. 'The back seat, Leo.'

At last, a bit of fairness.

We drive along the Gold Coast Highway. There are beaches, motels, more beaches, more motels, neon signs, more beaches, more motels. The airport. I point out a Cessna four-seater plane. 'I'm going to fly one of them one day.' Anna is impressed. 'I'll fly everyone to the Gold Coast.'

'Not me,' Rob calls out. 'Jack in the air sounds dangerous.'

'Dangerous? Sure. You're just scared. Scared Rob.'

'He's not.' Samantha sticks her tongue out at me. 'Rob isn't scared. DAD isn't scared of anything.'

Dad, Dad, Dad. Everyone calls Rob Dad, except me.

'That's my girl.' Rob laughs. 'My little Samantha.'

Samantha is HIS little girl. His girl. I tweak Samantha's pigtail. This all feels wrong.

Suddenly Mum turns around to look at me. 'And Jack is your boy, Rob, isn't he?'

Rob calls out. 'He sure is. My big, noisy boy.'

Mum adds, 'And Leo too.'

'Leo isn't as noisy as Jack, but you're all my kids.'

I stare at the back of Rob's head for a second. He has never said that before. Never.

Rob rubs his golf ball head. 'I'll have to wear a crash helmet when Jack is a pilot.'

Oh, he's joking. I shake my head. I call out, 'Mr Never-Scared crash-helmet rider, I've got a limerick.

Row row row your boat
Gently down the stream
Let's chuck Rob overboard
And listen to him scream.'

Everyone laughs, even Rob. Mum giggles. 'Come on kids, we'd have to pull him out of the stream. If he was thrown overboard, who'd drive us to the dolphins?'

'I will.' Samantha tickles the top of Rob's hair.

'Hey, don't touch.' Rob is very protective about his hair, especially when he's driving.

Tropical weather definitely makes plants grow — big green palms and lime green ferns, pink hibiscuses, bright red banksias, orange birds of paradise. Mum is in flower-power heaven. She is not very impressed with the bowling alley and the cinemas, shops and restaurants and even MORE motels. The motels are getting taller as we drive along — one storey, two storeys, five storeys, ten storeys, big skyscrapers, bigger skyscrapers. We hit Surfers Paradise.

'Look at that.' Samantha bends her head back so far it sounds like it's cracking. A giant bungee jump. I'd love to go on that. Wow.

I start laughing. There has definitely been an invasion of Hawaiian shirts into Surfers Paradise. They are everywhere. Eating breakfast in outdoor cafés, buying souvenirs in shops, walking around licking ice cream cones. There is music blaring from a beer garden even though it is still only the morning. Surfers Paradise is a party town. Two unconscious guys are sprawled out under a coconut palm tree. There are a few coconuts lying next to them, but we're not sure which ones are the nuts. Ha, ha.

Anna digs her elbow into me. 'Looks like they're a bit sick.'

'They remind me of Hector when I dyed him green.'
I turn around to get a better view. 'No, my rat looked
better.' Hope Christopher is looking after Hector
properly. 'Can we visit Surfers Paradise?' I hit Rob's
head. Oops, it was a bit hard. I'm just about to say
sorry when the car zooms forward in a mighty jump.

'You idiot, Jack.' Rob shouts at me right in front of
Anna, Leo and everyone. 'Not while I'm driving.' It
is a mean shout, a really mean one. He didn't have
to be mean and call me a name. Rob slows down.

'It was an accident, Rob,' I say.

Leo smirks. 'Yes. It was an accident, Dad.' What's
Leo playing at? Oh I know. He wants to look good.

Rob is rubbing his head. 'Okay, Leo. You're right.'

Leo, right? What is that about? I already told Rob
that it was an accident. Oh, but that's not good
enough. It's what Leo says that matters. Rob is Leo's
dad, not mine. Rob doesn't care what I say. He calls
us all his kids, but it doesn't look like it. My head is
throbbing. I am not talking to Rob any more.

Mum reaches out for my hand. 'Don't worry,
Jack.' That's why Mum is MY mum and Rob is not
my dad. 'You shouldn't have shouted at Jack,' she
says to Rob.

'Look, that was dangerous. I could have had an
accident.' Rob puts on this serious voice.

'It wasn't on purpose, Rob.'

I love Mum. She is right. I was just telling Rob
something. That was all. It WAS an accident.

111

'Jack can do no wrong, is that the way it is?'

That is so untrue. Rob doesn't know what he's talking about. Mum is always defending Rob, not me.

'I don't defend just Jack. I defend everyone in the family. You know that.' Mum and Rob stop talking.

Signs to the dolphins start appearing and the skyscrapers start disappearing. There are gardens and parks and Samantha insists on pointing out EVERY frangipani tree. I am not interested. I don't like Rob. He's not my dad. We drive beside a wide sandy bay dotted with boats at one end and surf beaches at the other end.

Mum turns around to me. 'Rob didn't mean to shout at you, Jack.' Mum is red. 'But you have to be more careful when someone is driving.'

I say nothing.

'Come on, Jack, we're going to have a good time.' Mum turns to Rob. 'Jack is sorry, Rob.'

Mum is always the peacemaker, even when everything is wrong. Sorry? I'm not sorry any more.

Samantha's wiggly hand is zooming around like a bee. I grab it and squeeze hard. 'Ouch.' Samantha throws a slap at me, which misses. Anna is sympathetic to Samantha's sore hand. As if it is really sore. Leo is sympathetic to Anna. This is all working out BADLY.

Rob parks. 'Dolphins,' he announces and walks around to my side of the car. Mum is helping Nanna out of the back seat. As I get out of the car,

Rob slouches over to me. I refuse to look at him. He speaks quietly. 'Jack.'

I still don't look.

'You shouldn't have hit my head while I was driving, Jack. But, well . . .' Rob stutters, 'I admit that I overreacted. When the car jumped, I got angry for a second.' He waits. 'People get angry, Jack.'

I squint at Rob. I'm not sure.

'Can we forget it? I was wrong.'

I nod.

He puts his arm on my shoulder. 'And I think you'll make a great pilot one day.'

Nanna is out of the car. That is the signal to head towards the entrance of the dolphin park. She has her stick raised ready to plant on the ground, when suddenly a gust of wind blows up her skirt. 'Oops.' She stumbles, landing on her hands with her bum in the air. 'Not hurt, not hurt,' she burbles.

We all stare for a second. She must have dozens of them. It is amazing. Big, purple, sparkling in the sun. Nanna's underpants shoot beams of light in all directions. We automatically duck. 'It's like a secret weapon.' I elbow Samantha. I don't want to, but a gurgle forces its way up my throat. There is a gurgle from Samantha too. Then Anna. We are all gurgling. Mum and Rob are holding hands laughing.

Poor Nanna.

Chapter 10

Anna's Silver Wings

Rob buys the entrance tickets and we race through the gates. Immediately Samantha spots a smiley-faced dolphin standing on his tail. Next thing, she is cuddling him, even though he is concrete. Nanna spots the concrete dolphin next and excitedly waddles towards it. She gives the smiley-faced dolphin a cuddle too. A Samantha–Nanna–dolphin group huddle is too good an opportunity to miss. I snap a photo.

'Fairy penguins,' Anna calls out, running towards them. I follow. Oh no. They waddle like Nanna. Ha, ha. These waddling midget penguins flap and somersault in and out of the water. 'They're so cute.' Anna hides her dimples behind her hands. She is the cute one. I snap a photo.

Suddenly a big fairy penguin is shuffling towards us. It is wearing a red hat and dinner suit. Samantha is shy and gives it a little wave. It waves back. 'Go on, give the penguin a hug.' Mum pushes Samantha towards him. Samantha just looks down at the ground, but Anna is brave. She laughs and hugs the big fairy penguin. Samantha shuffles towards them with Mum whispering in her ear. I snap another photo. Then I see the fairy penguin's flippers give them both a big squash, a really big squash. I get suspicious.

'Hey, who's in there?' I sneak a look through its permanent plastic smile. A tongue pokes out at me. I twist the penguin's red hat, until the penguin squeaks, 'Let go.'

'Did the penguin say something?' Anna asks.

'Yeah, goodbye.' We're getting out of here.

'Goodbye big fairy penguin.' Samantha gives him an extra cuddle.

I drag her away. 'That's one fishy penguin.'

'That's a very unfunny joke,' Samantha complains.

I don't answer, because the FISH word just popped out. Hope no one noticed. 'Monorail, this way.' I point. Everyone thinks that is a great idea except for the gigantic flight of stairs all the way up to it. Nanna. What is the point of her being here if she can't go on anything?

'I'll be right.' Nanna gets her walking stick into action, with Mum hovering behind her in case she topples backwards.

I am at the top already. I hang over the railing, calling out, 'Come on, come on. We'll miss it. We'll miss it.'

'Stop it, Jack.' Mum's hair frizzles. 'We've got all day.'

That's right — we have only one day. Nanna arrives at last. 'All aboard. Monorail. All aboard.' We get a cabin to ourselves. Excellent. We get a great view from the monorail. 'Oh, look at that.' The corkscrew rollercoaster zooms into loops. People are screaming. 'I'm going on it for sure. Triple loops.' It's fast. I nudge Anna. 'I reckon it's got to be 100 kilometres per hour.'

'Sure,' Leo snickers.

'What would you know? It IS fast.'

'I like fast rides.' Anna's angel wings quiver.

'Me too.' Samantha's nose is squished against the window pane. 'Dolphins,' she squeaks. 'Oh, look down there. In the lagoon.' Samantha touches her dolphin necklace. She wore it especially today. Anna and Samantha laugh and point at the dolphins diving into the water. Nanna tries to laugh too, but her teeth jerk forward. Oh, gross. She's taking them out. I wish she wouldn't do that, especially in front of Anna and Leo. Her face caves in and those pink plastic gums and false teeth look like Dracula has ripped them out. I groan. It's bad enough at night, when she leaves them in a glass of water. Once, when she was staying at our place, I nearly drank them. Phew, she's put them back in.

We do two circuits on the monorail before getting off. Mum helps Nanna to a seat at the dolphin lagoon under a shady viewing area. 'There'll be a show soon.'

'We'll sit here and look after your lunches, children. Go and have a good time.'

Yessssss. Good one, Nanna. 'Mum, Rob, can we go?' We charge off. 'To the Pirate Ship.'

We watch the Pirate Ship swinging in a huge arc for a while. 'Seventy-five degrees at least,' I announce. I give Leo a savvy look. 'It's a FACT.' He better not argue, because I really do know. There are advantages to being a scientist. I can estimate distance, height, speed with near-exact precision. Also, I read the brochure, but I am not telling anyone that.

'I'm not riding on it,' Samantha announces. 'It'll make me sick.' She holds her stomach. Anna is thinking about it.

'Come on. Don't be useless,' I argue with them. No, the girls won't go on it until I try it first. 'Leo, are you coming?'

He shakes his head.

'You're too scared.'

'I'm not.'

'Well come on, then.'

Anna interrupts. 'Jack, don't force him. It's only a ride.'

What a wimp. I'm not wasting any more time. I board the ship alone. I belt up and wait for it to start. The Pirate Ship begins moving. It's huge, whooshing left, then right, then left. Zoom. Hey, this is terrific. I don't grab on to the safety railing. I raise my hands high as the ship rockets into an enormous swing. I shout out to the girls every time I fly past.

Ride over. Too soon. That was fun. I run through the exit. 'You've got to have a go.'

Anna laughs, twirling her licorice curls at me.

'I'll sit between Samantha and you. You'll be fine. It's fantastic.' I snort at Leo, 'Leo, you can just stay here and watch. It'll be nice and safe.'

Leo follows us on board. He doesn't have much choice. Watching would be too embarrassing. The ride starts. Anna screams so much that I have to put my arm around her. I feel one of her silver wings on her back. A tingle runs along my arm. Leo is stuck between Samantha and a huge, tattooed bikie. Ha, ha.

We have three rides. Even Leo likes it. It is getting hot. We run back to the lagoon. 'Nanna, Nanna,' I puff, 'drinks.' She forages in her bag and produces four cans of lemonade. We finish them, then have to go again. Oh yes, 'Nanna are you having a good time?' She starts talking about dolphins. 'Sounds great. Let's go, go,' I shout. 'Log ride.' People are coming out of the boats drenched. 'Looks great.'

Nearly our turn. It is cold inside the tunnel as the boat splashes through the dark. It starts to move faster, faster. We race around loops and twirls. Faster, faster. 'Ahhhhhh . . .' Samantha's screams nearly split my eardrums.

We rocket down the chute and crash into a pool of water. We are dripping wet and Anna's angel wings can't flap. She looks so funny. 'What's the difference between a wet Anna and a dry angel?'

Anna isn't sure if she is happy about this and puts her hands on her hips. 'What is it?'

'Nothing, except water.'

Anna blushes. Samantha gets soppy. 'That's really nice, Jack.' I have no alternative but to rub Samantha's nose in my wet T-shirt, then run. 'I'll get you,' she shouts after me, but I run faster than Samantha and she is laughing by the time she catches up to me.

We dry off as we eat our sandwiches back at the lagoon. Nanna asks us twenty-three times, 'Are you cold? Shouldn't you change your clothes? Here are some dry T-shirts.' I am going to kill Nanna.

Then it comes to me in a flash. This is the right moment. I drag out the left-over bag of jelly snakes. I hid them at the bottom of the lunch bag. 'Does anyone want a snake?' I sneak a look at Leo. He's shuffling his feet.

Nanna isn't interested in our wet clothes any more. Pneumonia isn't important when there are jelly snakes around. I hand her a red one. Nanna's favourite.

'Where did you find them?' Samantha says as she stuffs a snake into her mouth.

Leo's really shuffling now. I let him sweat.

'Yes, where?' Anna's wings quiver.

I look at Rob. Will I tell?

'Where?' Samantha copies Anna.

I squint at Leo. 'Found them under the seat when I got in the car today,' I lie.

Leo breathes a sign of relief. I hand him a yellow snake and stare him right in the face. 'So why did you do it?' I whisper under my breath.

'I don't know.'

'You do know. It was so you could have them all to yourself.' I look at Nanna chewing through the red snake. I wonder if Leo gets it.

'Are you going to tell?' Leo looks nervously at Rob.

'No, not this time.' I look at Rob too. 'You owe me one now.'

'The show is starting.' Samantha nudges me. Three dolphins leap into the air in unison, then dive, before they jump up again, this time on their tails. 'Look at their white tummies.' Samantha rubs hers.

'Fatter than yours.' I tickle under her arms. 'Full of squid. Little squirmy squid that suck out your eyes.'

'Don't, Jack.' Samantha hits my hands. 'I hate it when you say that about the eyes.'

'Suck, suck, suck,' I tease.

There go the dolphins again, zooming into the air like grey torpedoes. One is throwing a ball with his nose. Oh no, they're playing water polo. The trainer looks like an idiot when the smallest dolphin dive-bombs him. Nanna is laughing. I take out my camera. Double exposures. Double the dolphins and double the Nannas. That will look good.

The trainers leave, the dolphins swim to other lagoons and Nanna stays. She is tired. How can she be tired? She has done NOTHING. 'I'll sit here and look at people walking by.'

Good, we're off to other rides. 'Bye, Nanna.'

'There are polar bears that way.' Anna points. 'They're so gorgeous.'

It's already late afternoon when Mum and Rob come to find us. We are coming out of the exploding Bermuda Triangle volcano when Mum's voice tinkles through the smoke. 'Found you. Are you kids hungry?'

What a question. 'Starving.'

We eat hot chips with tomato sauce as we lie on the grass beside the lake. Nanna is on a bench, of course. A big blob of tomato sauce drips onto her white blouse. Photograph. 'Don't, Jack.' Nanna raises her knobby hand. Sorry, photographers have to record everything, even tomato blobs. Snap. Rob is tickling Mum. Snap. Anna has tomato sauce on her chin. Snap. Nanna hides her walking stick. Snap. Samantha is lying on Rob's chest. Snap. Leo sits next to Rob. I don't take that picture.

Rob rubs Samantha's cheek. 'Time to leave.'

Samantha stretches and yawns. 'Oops, we forgot to visit the aquarium to see the tropical fish.'

Oh no, did Nanna hear that? Please, please don't tell the fish and pee-pee story in front of Leo. Please. Phew, Nanna is too busy telling Mum about her 'lost' walking stick. I know where she has hidden it.

'Here's your stick, Nanna.'

'Oh good, Jack.' Nanna twinkles.

Nanna is kidding.

Chapter 11

Rob has Shrunk

I dreamt about dolphins all night and slept like a stuffed cane toad. I look at my watch. It is already after nine in the morning. I climb down the bunk ladder, say hi to Leo, then check in the girls' room for the Samantha lump. Missing. Anna is missing too. I head for the bathroom. Oh no, war zone territory. Commander Mum is in battle dress, her hair pinned into a single twirl with bits escaping like gunfire. Samantha is her infantry troop. Anna is an onlooker. I stick my thumb up at Anna. Dirty clothes are everywhere. Mum is in action mode and Samantha is her action assistant. 'All clothes,' Mum orders as she zips through bags and piles of wet towels. Target, the laundry. Samantha dumps all the clothes in a pile on the floor and waits for Mum's instructions.

The problem is that Mum is not a great general when it comes to washing clothes. There is a bit of a brain drain with the basic moves. She doesn't separate whites and colours or fluffy and non-fluffy towels. At home, Mum hangs out my shorts upside down and folded in the middle. That's why when my shorts are dry and I am wearing them, there is always a crease line along my bum. Washing means that my T-shirts are dotted like the measles with white bits from the towels. Mum never measures how much soap powder to put in the machine. So sometimes our clothes come out of the wash stiff with dried soap. Other times, my clothes are clean but still marked with black lines from soccer slides.

Rob is different. He pegs every sock and handkerchief separately. There are no extra folds when he hangs his clothes on the line. His shirts are soft and smell good. He even measures the soap powder exactly. I have never seen his towels stiff. I think it's because he works in the spare parts warehouse and you have to be exact. Rob does his own washing. I wish he would do mine.

'Nanna, Nanna,' Samantha calls out. 'Need your washing.'

Nanna shakes her head. 'I haven't got any.'

There is a big stain in the middle of her white blouse from when she dropped tomato sauce on it yesterday. She tried to wash it. The stain doesn't look like tomato sauce any more. It's more like a grubby splotch. 'Nanna, your blouse is dirty. Can we wash it?'

Nanna presses her lips together and shakes her head. She knows Mum is a terrible washer, but Nanna can't do her laundry very well any more. There used to be a time when there were no sheets whiter than Nanna's, no clothes cleaner. Everyone knew Nanna was the best washer, but lately there are always spots on her clothes. She refuses to give Samantha her tomato sauce blouse.

'The clothes are in the washing machine, even Rob's,' Mum announces proudly. 'First load, anyway.' Mum smiles at Leo, who has just come out of his bedroom. He has unglued himself from his computer game. 'I'll put your clothes in the second wash.' He doesn't even answer her. Mum pretends it doesn't hurt her feelings. She bounces onto the couch next to Rob. 'It'll be dry before we go out this afternoon.'

This afternoon? What about now? We can't really be waiting for the washing. The sun is shining. How dumb is that? 'Can't we go before then?' I give Mum this doggy wide-eyed look.

Mum usually falls for it, but not today. She is in commander mode and pursuing her target.

'What did your mother say?' I hate it when Rob acts as if he is the back-up artillery.

'We'll wait until the washing is finished, Jack. No argument.' I can see Mum means it.

That is really great. NOT. Since Rob, Mum is losing it. AND the washing machine sounds like a crazed tornado. The machine is definitely unbalanced, but I refuse to put a wood block under it. I hope it crashes through the bath tub. I stomp over to Nanna, who is sitting in her chair. I bend down to give her a hug as I glance out of the window. The surf is rolling. Looking good. Very good. A bright idea strikes me. Hey, I'm not hanging around here listening to the washing machine. I yell out. 'Beach.'

There is scuffling. The washing infantry asks Mum if she is needed any more. 'No, no, Samantha darling, you've been a big help. Go for a swim.' Samantha and Anna grab beach towels. Leo grabs one too and we all move out.

Body surfing. I nearly get a perfect wave. Hey, Leo does too. Samantha is dumped. Ha, ha. There is sand all over her hair and I bet, up her nose. Ha, ha. Anna turns around and gives me a disappointed look. Oops, better stop laughing. I dive under a big wave. 'Come on.' I point out a set of smooth curls coming towards us. We turn to face shore then race into the swell, trying to catch waves that take us right in. No luck. I dive underwater and grab Samantha's legs when she isn't looking. Splash. Samantha is under. Anna jumps me and I drag her under too. Girls spluttering, ha, ha, until they both leap at me and I'm down and out. They are laughing now.

'Drowned rat.' Anna splashes water at me.

'You look like Hector's twin.' Samantha splashes me too.

We have the best water fight, until Anna escapes onto the beach. Samantha follows her. Anna flicks her towel in the air. I look at my waterproof watch. 'We'd better get back.'

'I want to stay.' Leo dives into the surf.

'Well, stay,' I yell, then start walking back.

'Stop, Jack. We've got to wait for him.' Anna sits on her towel. Samantha sits next to her. Ganging up. I hate that.

'Why? Leo doesn't need us watching him.' I slump beside them. 'He wouldn't wait for us.'

'You don't know that.' Anna shakes her head. 'It's hard to join in without knowing anyone.'

'He knows us and Rob is his dad. He ignores Mum and doesn't even like Nanna.'

'Well, maybe he just wanted to be with Rob.' Anna flattens the sand in front of her. 'He could be jealous.'

'Jealous? Of what?'

'You. Samantha and you live with Rob. Leo isn't part of it.'

'Well, he's on holidays with us, isn't he?'

'That's not the same as living with you all.' Anna presses her finger against her dimple. I don't know.

We hang around and I keep looking at my watch. Then I start telling jokes. Good ones about sharks and surfers at the beach. 'Hey, what do dolphins have that no other animals have?'

'Don't know.'

'Baby dolphins.'

The girls are laughing, and finally Leo splashes out of the surf. We clump into the apartment with wet towels. 'More washing. Great surf, you should go out,' I tell Mum, who is standing in the kitchen. Mum has weird pinkish splotches on her face. 'Are you all right?' Mum doesn't answer. I look at Nanna, who is sitting in her chair hiding a creased, crinkled smile. This is suspicious. 'What's wrong?'

Suddenly Rob appears in the doorway. Our mouths open in amazement. He is standing there with his skinny legs and bumpy knees. No one usually sees his bumpy knees, but we do today. His shorts are edging up his bum crack and they are tight. Really tight. His T-shirt is glued to his body and reaches just above his belly button. His shorts and T-shirt match. They are both khaki. Brown, pooey khaki.

Nanna is the first to break. Her crinkles stretch into a cheery smile. Anna is nearly wetting herself. Samantha has to run to the bathroom. I am cracking up. Leo is too. Rob is laughing. There is only one person who isn't. MUM.

Samantha is out of the bathroom. She makes a grand entrance, then doubles over giggling. She flashes more evidence of disaster. Baby-sized T-shirts, green and white striped towels that are multicoloured now, pygmy underpants. Samantha's favourite white heart nightie is green. It's lucky that Rob's socks have been saved. They must be made of elastic. They haven't shrunk. They've just turned greeny-brown. Anna runs into the bedroom. Phew, she is back with her angel T-shirt. It didn't go into the first load. Saved.

Poor Mum. She forgot to turn the water temperature to COLD. Boiling hot water, dye-running green beach towels, an extra long wash, mixed colours. By the end of the wash, everything was clean. It's just that everything was different. Small, shrunk and poo-coloured.

Nanna keeps smiling and touching her tomato sauce blouse. She loves that blouse. Clever Nanna.

Poor Mum has to listen to washing jokes all through lunch, then as we pile into the car, and later as we head towards the water park. There are breakouts of spontaneous hooting. 'What are small, rolly and brown?' Ha, ha, ha. 'Rob's socks.'

We arrive. Mum finally cracks. Her cheeks are giant splotches now. Her voice is nails scraping on the blackboard. 'NO MORE WASHING JOKES.' Then she breaks into a sob. 'I'm sorry.' Poor Mum. Rob puts his arms around her. So does Samantha. There is a group hug. Yeah, yeah, but I can hear splashing, see water slides. Aren't we over this?

I tug Samantha's T-shirt. 'Mum, it's okay. Let's go.' Rob and Mum hold hands. I don't care. Let's move. I smell water.

Change rooms at last. I whistle when Anna comes out in a light blue sparkly bikini. New swimmers. Anna got them for Christmas and has been saving them. She looks fantastic. I whistle at Samantha too. She is wearing her yellow sparkly bikini. Sparkles must be in. Leo says he thinks they look fantastic too, but it was ME who whistled first.

Then Nanna arrives. I try to whistle, but it's pretty difficult when you see Nanna. She loves flowers like Mum does, but even Mum wouldn't wear this. It is Nanna's new swimming costume. She has a big, no, I mean a GIANT swimming costume on. That doesn't even worry me. It is the colour, the pattern. There are massive green, blue and red flowers all over it. Two giant leaves act as the straps to hold up the whole contraption. The worst is an evil yellow snapdragon on Nanna's stomach. When she laughs, the snapdragon sneers, snarls, then snaps. Scary stuff. Samantha is giggling behind her hand. 'Smile, Nanna.' She does. The snapdragon snaps and I click a photograph.

Mum is wearing her usual blue daisy swimmers. Thank goodness they weren't shrunk in the wash. There is a great effort made by everyone to unload Nanna into the giant wave pool. She has left her walking stick in the car, but she doesn't need it in the pool, she says. I am sick of her stupid walking stick, anyway. I'm not going back to get it. No way. It must be one of Mum's weak moments. 'Nanna doesn't need it now.' Nanna ends up happily floating on an inflatable tyre, bobbing up and down with Mum floating next to her. The rest of us head off. There is serious fun out there.

I see it. A high-speed, four-storey, forty-five degree plunge. Death defying. I don't even bother asking anyone else. 'Rob, Rob. Are you coming?'

'Leo, do you want to have a go?' Rob asks.

As if he would. What about me? I want to go with Rob. No, Leo doesn't want to ride. Good.

We climb the steps, up, up, up. 'Be careful, Jack.' Anna's voice peters out as we battle to the top. I stick my thumb up at the girls, who look like shrunken dolls. It is a long, long way down to the splash pool. We watch toboggans speed down the slide, with people's mouths open and screams breaking eardrums.

I am having second thoughts when the attendant shoves us to the start. Rob is at the front. I am clinging on to him. 'I don't know about . . .' The attendant presses the shove button and 'Aaahhhh . . .' we're double screaming.

Anna clicks a terrific photo of us. The ride was unbelievable but Rob doesn't want to have another go. That's okay, because we have lots of other things to do.

We race around like maniacs from one slide to another. Anna and Samantha cling to each other on a water rage turner that spirals in total darkness. I click them with their mouths wide open as they hurtle into the exit pool. 'Scared?' I yell at them. They splutter and splatter, emerging like drowned bunnies. Can you believe it? They are doing it again.

'Come on.' It is white water territory. We climb into a raft with water breaking over the sides, then there is the plunge, wild water and earsplitting shrieks as we go over the falls. Anna holds on to me as we spin down rapids and smash into turns. We are soaking wet and laughing, dripping out of the raft. Anna shakes her hands at me, scattering drops into my face. 'You're on, Anna.' I pick her up and swirl her around until she is begging me to stop. No stopping. Twirl, tickle, twist.

We are falling over each other in a heap when Leo twirls Anna away. 'Safe.' He smiles.

Anna thanks him 'for saving me from the Jack'.

I've had it with that jerk. When Leo heads off to the toilets, I follow him. I grab his skinny arm and drag him around the back of the toilets.

'What's up?' he asks.

'I'll tell you what's up. I'm sick of you trying to impress Anna and making me look bad.'

'Why? Do you like her?'

'Yeah, I do. She's my friend.'

'Well, she's my friend too.'

'What's your problem, Leo?' It spurts out of me like bad milk. 'You're always sneering at me. You sneer at Mum too. Like, what's she done to you? Why did you steal the jelly snakes? And you're mean to Nanna. She's nice to you.'

'Yeah, real nice. She wants me to wear purple underpants. That sounds great,' he scoffs.

'Stop it.' I shove my face so close to his that our eyeballs are nearly touching. 'My nanna is kind to you. Kind. My whole family and Anna are kind to you.' A volcano is exploding inside my head.

'Yeah, who is YOUR family? Does that include MY dad? Rob is MY dad.' He shoves me. 'He's not YOUR dad.'

I shove him in the chest. 'Well, I haven't got a dad. So you're lucky, aren't you?'

'Sure, except I never see him.' He kicks the ground. 'You see him all the time. You do stuff with him. Stuff I don't even know about.' Leo is spitting out words. 'Like thermometers.'

'Thermometers? What are you talking about?'

'You think about it if you can. I'm going to the toilet now, if that's okay with you.'

My head is throbbing as I walk away.

Anna and Samantha are waiting. Mum has arrived too. 'Nanna had enough of the wave pool. She's on a bench waiting for us to come back. She's a bit tired.'

'Here comes Leo.' Rob waves at him.

That's a real thrill. Leo is here. Whoopee-doo.

'Hi, Nanna.' She waves at us but she is shaking a bit. I feel shaky too. The snapdragon on her stomach wiggles.

'Are you cold?' Mum puts Nanna's towel around her to stop her shakes.

'I'm fine, everyone. Don't fuss.'

'Maybe it's time to go home now, kids.'

'Home?' Samantha's face drops like a deflated balloon.

I look up. The sun is starting to set already.

'Can we stay just a bit longer, Mum? Pleasssse?' Samantha yanks Mum's skirt.

Nanna sparkles a smile. 'Let them have another ride.'

'Well, if Nanna doesn't mind.' Mum looks at her, then us, then her. 'Half an hour only, and that's it.'

Nanna takes out her last cookie from her bag. She'll be happy with that.

Samantha runs ahead with Leo and Anna. I walk behind. I'm not going on any more water slides and grab my camera. I need time to calm down. Suddenly Samantha starts yelping, jumping up and down like an elastic band. I run over straightaway. 'Are you all right? Are you, Samantha? Stop screaming. What?' Samantha is pointing excitedly at a pink hibiscus bush. Then I see it bouncing under the bush. I pull Samantha's pigtail. 'You're a great sister. Shushhhh.' It stops dead still trying to blend into the twigs.

'What is it?' Anna whispers. We slowly move towards it. Anna gasps.

It's warty and brown with cream speckles and has huge horizontal eyes. Got to be twenty centimetres long. 'Big one,' I whisper. 'A kilo at least.' I've never seen one alive. 'Cane toad. Eats bugs, especially in sugar cane plantations.' Quietly I pull out my camera. Click. Oh no. It's moving. Click. It's on the go, fast, faster, racing for the undergrowth.

'Yuck,' the girls say together, speeding in the opposite direction. Leo chases after them.

I stay behind, quietly hoping the cane toad will come back. It doesn't.

Chapter 12

The Hero

Nanna is wobbly as she hobbles towards the exit in her snapdragon swimmers. She has her towel still around her shoulders and is shuffling forward in rubber sandals. Nanna's toes twinkle when she isn't wearing her orthopaedic lace-up shoes and her hands dance without her stick.

I glance at Anna. I get this buzzing feeling inside. Her hair is amazing when it's wet. It tangles into springy curls.

I am just about to open the car door for her when suddenly there is a huge bang, then this long moan. I turn around. It's Nanna. She is on the ground with her snapdragon swimmers stretched into a horrible grin. Her face is crinkled into this desperate gasp for air. As I rush over I see her green eyes flicker, then close.

'It's all right, it's all right,' Mum stammers, but it's not all right. It is different from the fall in the dolphin car park. There is blood dribbling from the back of her head. Vomit trickles out of the corner of her mouth.

'Nanna, Nanna.' Samantha is crying.

Nanna's lips tremble, then spasm. 'She's not breathing,' Mum shouts. 'Call emergency. Emergency.' Rob is already on his mobile.

'Nanna's stopped breathing.' Samantha sobs.

Rob keeps repeating on the phone. 'Urgent, urgent. Not breathing. Urgent.'

Everything is happening so fast. My heart is thudding. I push Mum out of the way and roll Nanna onto her side. My fingers are in her mouth, grabbing her teeth, pulling her tongue forward, clearing the vomit.

Mum is hitting Nanna's back. 'Breathe, breathe,' she whispers.

I gulp down my panic. Nanna needs me. I know how to do this. I've done first aid at school. I have to do it for my nanna. I roll her flat, push my hand under her neck, tilt her head back. Okay Jack, okay. I have to be calm. I push her chin down and take a deep mouthful of air. I puff breath into Nanna's mouth, wait, puff, wait, puff, when suddenly she starts coughing, then moving. 'Nanna,' I whisper. 'Nanna.' Her eyes blink open, then shut, but she is breathing.

The ambulance sirens scream to a halt. I am pushed out of the way, shaking. Samantha runs to hug me. Anna presses her head against my back. Mum is talking to the ambulance paramedics with Rob standing beside her. Nanna is whimpering as they lift her onto the stretcher. Mum comes over to me, hugs me, whispering in my ear. 'Thank you, Jack. Thank you, darling.' She gives a quick wave as she climbs into the back of the ambulance.

Rob tells me to get into the front seat of the car. 'Leo, you get into the back.'

'But Dad . . .'

'Get into the car.' Rob nearly shouts.

Leo slams the car door. I squint at him. I don't care about Leo. Nanna could have died.

We follow the ambulance, charging to the hospital. It screeches into Emergency. Rob swerves into the car park. I am starting to get out when Rob orders everyone to stay in the car. 'But Rob . . .'

He doesn't let me finish. 'There are too many of us for the Emergency Room. Can you all stay here? Jack, could you take charge?'

I want to go inside. It was me who saved Nanna. Me. I want to argue, but Rob has already sprinted away. He turns around, raises his thumb, then disappears into the hospital. Then we wait, wait, wait. I bite my lip until I feel it cutting into my mouth. I see Nanna's white face and the rickle of blood. My nanna, my nanna.

Anna whispers, 'You're a hero, Jack.'

I whisper, 'I'm not.'

'You are, Jack.' Samantha rests her head against my shoulder.

Leo mumbles, 'It was good, Jack.'

I glance at Leo. I start to shake. I want to cry, but I know I can't. Not here. I blow out quick puffs of air. Swallow hard. Calm down, calm down.

It is ages before Rob comes back. 'Nanna is going to be fine.' He gets into the driver's seat. 'Mum will stay here until the doctors sort out what to do. It'll take a while.' He turns on the ignition. 'I'll drop you kids at the apartment, then get back here.'

Nanna and Mum need me. 'I'm going to the hospital with you, Rob.' I shift in my seat.

Rob turns to look at me. 'What you did for your Nanna, I couldn't have done it.' He coughs. 'No, more than that. I didn't do it. You did.' He turns out of the car park. 'Jack, please can you stay with Samantha and Anna and Leo? It'll make your mum and me feel better.'

I have to. 'All right.'

As soon as Rob gets back to the apartment, he rummages through Nanna's clothes and finds a jacket to take her. He gets a jumper for Mum. 'I'll phone you from the hospital. There's dinner. Pizza in the fridge.' He hands me his mobile phone. 'Call the hospital if there's anything you want.' Rob programs the hospital number into the phone.

Samantha runs up to him. He brushes her cheek. 'I'll phone you as soon as I know what's happening.'

No one is hungry. Anna keeps talking about the fall, Nanna's white face, the vomit sliding from the edge of her mouth. 'Wasn't it terrible to give her mouth-to-mouth?'

I nod. I didn't taste the vomit then, but afterwards I did. I had to concentrate on blowing air into Nanna's lungs. 'I just wanted to save her.'

'You did, Jack. You did.' Anna hugs Samantha.

Leo says nothing.

We get a bit hungry later and eat the pizza. We watch TV, play dominoes and Leo's computer games. He lets us have a go for the first time. I keep looking at the kitchen clock. Why is it taking so long? Is Nanna really all right? We look out of the lounge room window, watch more TV.

It has been nearly three hours when the phone rings. I grab it first. Anna and Samantha squash next to me trying to hear.

'Nanna has a fracture in her wrist. No, she doesn't need surgery . . . Yes, it has to have a plaster . . . No, not a full plaster, only a half one . . . Yes, she's cut the back of her head. She's had some stitches . . . Yes, she has to stay in hospital for a few days. We'll be home soon.'

'Yes,' I shout. 'Nanna is all right.' Samantha and Anna dance around the room. I'm laughing at them. 'Are you rubber balls?' That's the sign for them to jump on me. 'You're squashing me,' I yell out, but they keep squashing until I shout, 'Give in, give in.'

Suddenly headlights beam through the lounge room window. Samantha is still jumping. Leo calls out, 'They're here.'

Mum looks exhausted, with her blonde hair frazzled and her daisy skirt crushed. Rob forces her to sit in Nanna's lounge chair. She smiles at us. 'Nanna is all right. Don't worry.'

'What really happened, Rob?'

'Nanna was shivering and tired at the pool. When she got to the car she was weak and started coughing. She coughed up the cookie she'd been eating. The pieces got caught in her throat and stopped her breathing.'

Rob brings Mum a cup of coffee and some left-over pizza. She doesn't eat the pizza. Mum says that she will stay with Nanna tomorrow.

'I'll go in with you to the hospital.' Samantha sits on the floor next to her.

We all want to visit.

'We'll see. You are such special kids. I'm so proud of you all, especially Jack.' Mum reaches for my hand. 'Nanna stopped breathing. Nanna . . . Jack, you saved her life.' A shiver runs through me. 'She's going to be fine because of you.'

It has been a long day. The girls are in the bathroom. I hear the blow dryer buzzing away. I head towards the kitchen. Mum and Rob are sitting at the bench talking. Mum is rubbing her lips. 'We have to do something about Nanna.' Mum makes a sobbing sound. 'She's always been there for us.' The honey scent of the frangipanis on the bench is so strong. I rub my nose. 'She just can't live by herself any more. She can't.' Mum has tears in her eyes. They don't see me, so I quietly back away.

Anna talks to her parents on the phone, telling them every detail about Nanna. The Napolis love Nanna, so I hear lots of bellissimas and grande Nanna expressions bellowing down the line. Then Leo phones his mother. He always has these strange conversations with his mum about what Rob is supposed to be doing. It's like she wants us to be unhappy. Maybe it's because she is unhappy. I don't know. My head is aching. I have to go to bed. I feel under the bunk bed and drag out my fungus. The growths take up nearly the whole jar now. They look like alien flowers. Have I created a new life form? I'd really like to do that. Suddenly I think of Nanna with her snapdragon swimming costume. She could have died. I slide my fungus back under the bunk, then climb the bunk ladder. I lie on my back looking at the ceiling.

Anna and Samantha stick their heads into my room. 'Goodnight Jack.'

Leo must have finished his phone call. He is probably playing his computer games in the lounge room.

Mum tiptoes into my bedroom. 'How are you feeling?' Her daisy smile appears over the bunk railing.

'I don't know.' I gulp.

'Everything is going to be fine now.' She kisses me.

'Mum?'

'Yes, Jack?'

'You won't send Nanna away, will you?'

Mum hesitates. 'I don't want to, Jack, but . . .' Mum kisses me again.

Rob's voice booms through the apartment. 'Goodnight Anna.'

'Goodnight Rob.'

'Goodnight Samantha. Sleep tight and don't let the bed bugs bite.'

There are Samantha giggles. ''Night, Dad.'

Dad? I bury my face in my pillow. I want Rob to be my dad. I just do.

'Goodnight Jack.'

I want to call him Dad. 'Goodnight Rob.' I am so tired.

I hear Rob talking to Leo. 'Computer games . . . winning . . . that man out . . .'

Zzzzzzzzzzzz.

Chapter 13

Tower of Terror

Next morning Mum insists that we are still going out, even if Nanna is in hospital. 'You can't help her anyway.' Mum is packing lunch for us. 'I'll stay with Nanna today.' She tilts her head to the side. 'Rob's happy to take you kids out. He loves rollercoaster rides, don't you?'

'Right.' Rob rubs Mum's cheek.

We run through the hospital corridors looking for Nanna. Anna is wearing her silver wings again and looks like she's flying. There is a nervous knot in my stomach as we get near Nanna's ward. She was so pale when she collapsed. I feel scared inside for her.

'Here, here,' Samantha squeals as she turns into a ward. There are six hospital beds with five other ladies and Nanna. She is lying flat except for two pillows under her head. The back of her head is bandaged and her puffed hair has a hole in it. Luckily Nanna can't see it. Her left wrist is in plaster. When she notices us, her face breaks into a crinkly smile. She looks much better. My stomach unknots and it's easier to breathe. There is careful kissing because Nanna says she is sore. There are bruises down her leg. Poor Nanna

Nanna strokes Anna's silver wings with her good hand. 'Pretty,' she grins. I am so glad Mum didn't wash Anna's T-shirt.

Nanna yawns and Mum tells us that we better leave. 'But we just got here, Mum.'

'I love theme parks.' Nanna's green eyes twinkle. 'You have to have a good time for me there.' I'm not sure about this. Samantha snuggles beside me. Then Nanna stretches her good hand out to both of us. 'Please go. It'd make me happy.' She holds up her broken wrist. 'And I need to rest today.'

I hug Nanna, then Samantha and Anna do. Nanna smiles. 'Leo, come on. Give me a hug too.'

Leo presses his cheek against Nanna's. It's like watching a stick cuddling cotton wool. Nanna is the cotton wool. Rob puts his arm on Leo's shoulder and smiles.

This is getting crazy. Can't Rob see that Leo doesn't want us? Leo doesn't want Nanna to hug him.

Suddenly Nanna notices Rob's socks. 'Those socks,' she grins. They are the poo ones. We all start laughing, except for Mum.

'These socks are comfortable. I never liked white socks anyway.' Rob winks at me.

Mum shakes her head. 'That was a terrible wash. At least I didn't shrink you kids or Rob.' Mum bends down and pats Rob's socks. 'Go. Go. I don't want to see those socks here any more.'

Rob laughs. 'All right. All right. The socks are leaving.' Rob piggy-backs Samantha all the way to the car. 'Nanna is going to be fine.'

I know that is true, even though Nanna's head is bandaged and her hair wrecked. 'Hey, do you remember when I did Hector's hair?'

'Poor Hector. Not even a rat deserves that.' Anna twiddles her licorice curls.

'He didn't mind. I gave him extra cheese.'

Samantha asks Rob to put on a tape — rock. There aren't any moans. We are relieved Mum isn't in control of the music for once.

It's late morning already as we drive towards the theme park. Suddenly we see it, standing out on the horizon like a castle. 'Looks fantastic.' Samantha sticks her tongue out of the side of her mouth, concentrating. I try to grab it, but she is fast. Her tongue is back in her mouth quicker than a blink.

We park, load Mum's sandwiches and drinks into my backpack, put on our hats and sun cream.

Samantha grabs Rob's hand and I grab my camera. A big fat two-metre-tall koala gives a furry wave. We are definitely in the right place.

Map open. That must be the signal for everyone to shove their heads over my shoulder. It is very annoying. Problems. Anna points to the paddle wheeler. 'I'd love to go on that.' Then Samantha's stubby finger discovers the lagoon, but I have been hanging out for the Tower of Terror. The fastest, tallest ride in the world. Leo wants the dodgem cars. We are arguing when Samantha interrupts. 'Got to go.'

'Why didn't you go BEFORE we left the hospital?'

Samantha just turns up her nose at me. 'I have to wee, so there.' She begs Anna to go with her. I don't think girls can go to the bathroom alone.

While Rob, Leo and I stand around doing nothing, I notice Bengal Tigers on the map. '*There are only about 400 white tigers left in the whole world,*' I read from the information leaflet. As Samantha and Anna run towards us, I shout, 'Tigers, tigers.' There is giggly excitement. Yes, they want to see them. We all do. Agreed.

'Look, look,' Samantha squeaks when we get there. Two striped tigers are lolling around under the trees. Two white ones are rumbling with their keepers in a clearing.

Anna leans over the railing. 'The tigers are beautiful.' She flashes her dimples and quivers her wings. Meltdown. I flash my gappy smile at her.

'I wish the tigers were free.' Anna presses her lips together.

'They're endangered.' Rob rests on the railing overlooking the moat that separates the tigers from us. 'The breeding program helps them survive.' Samantha stands close to Rob, of course. 'But it would be great if they were free.' The tigers wrestle each other and the big one gets flattened. 'Now, one of those tigers reminds me of Jack.' Rob pushes his hands together. 'The squashed one,' he jokes.

I swing a few air punches at him. He blocks my attack. Samantha squeals, 'Don't hurt Rob!' which makes Rob call out, 'My little girl.'

Little girl? What a crawler. I take another swipe at Rob. He laughs and we tussle with each other, then Leo joins in. There are a few more defensive moves and attacks when Samantha grabs Rob's hand. 'Rides, Rob. Rides.' He is being dragged away when Leo takes a swipe that nearly gets me.

'Hey, what are you doing? You could have hit me.'

'Well, I didn't.'

I squint at him. I'm not sure about that.

We all end up on the swinging aerial chair rides, flying to nowhere. I rock my swing so that I nearly zap Samantha. She squiggles. 'Don't, don't, Jack.' So I do it again. Zap. Squeal. Zap. Squeal. This is fun.

The ride is over and Rob and I make a pact. We are going to stand up against the opposition. That is Anna and Samantha. 'The Tower of Terror next.'

They start to argue. 'What about the . . .'

'Tower of Terror time is now. If you don't want to ride the best thriller out, then you'll have to just watch.' I poke Samantha's arm. 'Don't break your neck looking up. It's only thirty-eight storeys high.'

As we all march towards the tower, Samantha blurts out, 'As if you'd go on that. Look at it.'

It's hard to miss the eleven-metre-high, crimson-eyed, metallic skull over the entrance. I squint at Rob. 'It's nothing.' I stick my thumb up at the girls. 'We're going to ride.'

'Leo, are you coming?' Rob asks.

He shuffles a bit.

'He doesn't have to, if he doesn't want to.' Anna stands next to him with her wings flapping. Leo stays with the girls and I'm relieved. This is Rob's and my ride.

Rob and I walk inside this maze of concrete and steel. There are huge crevasses and killing steel traps. One slip and we've had it. The launch pad at last. We line up to get inside the escape pod, a six-tonne steel case. We slide into the seats and buckle up. Warnings come over the intercom. Okay, okay. It's making me nervous now. I'll never admit it, though. Come on. Locked in. Start. Whoosh. We're blasted like jet-propelled cannons upwards fast, very fast. Over 160 kilometres per hour in seven seconds. The screams are deafening. My stomach. Where is it? We hit the top. Phew. Oh no, what's happening? We're falling, freefalling backwards like we're airborne, weightless spacemen. More screaming. My stomach. Landed stomach first, Jack second.

'That was some trip,' Rob says as we clamber shakily out of our pod.

'Some trip.' I pretend to punch Rob in the arm and he grabs my fist. He has me in an arm lock as we exit.

'It was the best.' The girls don't believe me.

'Leo, you missed out on a great ride,' I whisper under my breath. I don't call him a loser, but that's what I think he is.

We race to catch the train. Just in time. It puffs through the eucalyptus trees. The grass is really dry. Hot weather and no rain. Firetrap territory, if you ask me. Train stop. This is koala country, with the odd man-eating crocodile.

Samantha discovers the kangaroos. I don't know why she always gets so excited when she sees them. It is not like there aren't heaps of them hopping through the countryside. We nearly got killed once, when a big grey kangaroo raced across the road. Mum just missed it, otherwise we'd be dead (and it would, too). 'You're choking that kangaroo, Samantha.' She sticks out her tongue at me. Photo opportunity.

'I'm not.' Samantha keeps choking.

Anna and Leo pat them too. 'See the joey's head poking out of the pouch?'

The girls drag us over wooden bridges through gum trees and koala sanctuaries, past dingoes and fat-bummed wombats. The emus look like brooms with heads on them. Ha, ha. One of them pecks Samantha's head. She screams and does a dash behind Rob, who is laughing as well. Samantha isn't impressed.

Leo flashes a stuffed kangaroo at us. 'I won it.' He gives it to Anna.

'Thank you so much, Leo.' She has to be kidding.

My stomach is rumbling. The koalas are munching gum leaves. The dingoes are ripping into bones. The rosellas are pecking at birdseed. That fat wombat is burrowing into a hole. I bet he's found something juicy. I'm hungry. I rub my stomach. 'Food,' I pant. Pit stop. Mum's sandwiches save me from starvation. Leo doesn't like them, so Rob gives him money to get a hamburger. Rob isn't looking that happy about it. Leo is starting to lose points with him. At last.

The girls are still eating, but I've finished. I go off to check out where Leo has got to. He is not at the kiosk. I scratch my head and wander around looking for him. Where is he? Suddenly I notice the yellow cap. It flickers between the trees away from the pathway. Quietly I creep towards him. He is hunched over a hole with a half-eaten hamburger sticking out of his pocket. He's piling dry leaves into the hole. I just watch. His back is turned to me as I tread softly towards him. 'Got you,' I shout in his ear. He jumps, his mouth open in surprise. 'What are you doing, Leo?'

'Nothing.'

I kick the pile of leaves. 'Doesn't look like nothing.'

'Well, it is.'

'You idiot.'

'I wasn't doing anything.'

'Yeah. Right. Were you going to light that?'

'With what?' He shows me his empty hands then gives me the finger.

'I've seen your silver lighter.'

'It's my grandfather's. It's old.' Leo suddenly stops.'Anyway it's none of your business, Jack.'

'Well, if you were going to light a fire, you'd be a rat.'

'As if I would. What do you take me for?'

'I don't know,' I mutter under my breath. I'm going to keep an eye on him.

We walk back to our lunch spot. Is Leo telling the truth? Should I say something to Rob? He'll take Leo's side. I'm not sure about the lighter either. Leo saunters up to Rob like nothing happened. Maybe it was nothing or maybe not.

Samantha is hopping around like a kangaroo. She is excited because we are on our way to the lagoon. I glance at Leo. I shrug and follow Anna's silver wings. We wind through a replica of a dormant volcano dotted with tropical palms and water slides. Rob finds a comfortable spot and stretches out. We hit the water. A little girl attaches herself to Samantha and ends up swirling with her in a big rubber tyre.

Anna asks Leo to come with us on the big water slide. Wish she hadn't. We climb the steps up to the top. 'Go on, Leo. You go first,' I insist.

'That's nice, Jack.' Anna smiles.

Yeah, it's really nice. Getting rid of Leo. I wait for a few people to slide before us. Then Anna slides, with me following her and splashing from side to side with water gushing everywhere. We splash together in the pool, laughing.

I take Anna's hand and pull her out of the water. 'Let's do it again.' I hold her hand all the way to the top of the slide.

Chapter 14

Swimming with Friends

It's late when we get to the hospital ward. Mum waves, but Nanna is asleep. That is, until we come in. She must have some special sixth sense, because she suddenly opens her eyes. 'Oh, you're here.' She jiggles forward in her bed. 'Come over, Leo and Anna. Don't stand at the back.'

'Nanna, your hair looks great.' I don't mention the bandage at the back of her head.

'It does, it does.' Samantha squiggles onto the bed.

Leo rolls his eyes, but doesn't dare say anything standing next to Anna. Anna loves Nanna.

Nanna beams. 'A hairdresser in the hospital did it for me this afternoon.' This means that Nanna is really better.

'Your hair is nearly as good as when Stanley does it.' Samantha flicks her pigtails upwards.

'Who loves Stanley?' I tease Nanna.

Nanna blushes. She really does love Stanley. He makes a big fuss of her when she sees him. Stanley is the one who makes Nanna's hair hard. Every week he washes it, puts it in rollers then under a hair dryer, combs it and teases it into a puff before spraying it HARD. I've watched the whole process for scientific purposes.

'Do you remember when you made Hector's hair like Nanna's?' Samantha nudges me.

'Actually it was an experiment — as you know, Samantha.' I gave Hector a shampoo, a dye (green) and a blow dry. I used miniature curlers, but he didn't like them. He didn't seem to mind his hair being puffed up. I sprayed him until he was hard. He didn't like that much. Samantha assisted and held him down by his paws and tail. Samantha said he looked beautiful. As if that is the point. I was testing the effect of hard hair on my experimental rat. There was a bit of hair loss, but it grew back. Samantha was right, though. Hector looked good as a green fluffed-out hard rat.

Nanna isn't very interested in Hector. She's talking to Anna. 'I'll be out of hospital tomorrow.'

'That is so good, Nanna.'

'It is.' She beams.

We tell Nanna all about the theme park. She likes hearing about the tigers. 'Can you believe that Rob and Jack went on the Tower of Terror? Scary.' The girls do a duo shudder.

'Can I take a picture?' Nanna isn't sure, but Mum pats down the bandages at the back of Nanna's head. 'You look great.' Click. A photo with Mum, Rob and Leo next to her with her broken wrist extended like a trophy. Click. Another with Samantha and Anna kissing her cheeks on either side of her bandaged head. Click. 'Nanna, smile.' Click. Her teeth slide forward. I laugh. 'You look like Dracula.'

Nanna laughs too. 'Jack, I drink tea, not blood.' She grins. 'Well, maybe it's tea with a little bit of blood.'

'Yuck, Nanna.' Samantha wheezes. Yep, I definitely get my humour from Nanna.

When we say goodbye, Nanna suddenly stops smiling. 'My wrist hurts. My head hurts.' She wants Mum to stay. 'Don't leave yet.'

Mum takes the flower from behind her ear and puts it in Nanna's hair. 'I'll collect you tomorrow. Promise.' As we walk out of the ward, I feel awful. Nanna is trying not to cry. 'We'll be back soon.' Mum runs out of there. I do too.

Dinner is quiet tonight. Mum twiddles a frangipani until it looks like it needs resuscitation. 'We have to do something about Nanna,' she stammers, then shakes her head. 'I'm glad you all had a great time today.'

We talk about the tigers for a while, but I'm tired. 'I'm going to bed.' I give Mum a kiss, then rub Rob's prickly head. 'Golf head.' I laugh.

'Hey, don't touch.' Rob pretends to pat it down. 'Go to bed then, Jack.'

'Goodnight everyone.'

Bathroom. Brush teeth. I am never too tired to do that. I think of Nanna's false teeth. I shudder. Bedroom. Pyjamas on. Oh, must check my fungus. I reach under the bunk. Hey, it's not there. I fossick about. Where is it? Has the jar moved? Phew, found it. The green colour is amazing.

What? The mushroom growths are smaller. The fungus has shrunk. It can't have just collapsed like that. This is wrong, really wrong. Then I see it. Sand in the jar. Lots of it. Gold Coast sand. How did it get there? I slump against the wall with my jar in my lap.

Leo is standing at the door with this funny look. I glare up at him. I know Leo did it. I just know it. 'Was it you?'

'What are you talking about?' Leo starts to get into his pyjamas.

'The fungus. You did it, didn't you?'

'What?' Leo's face is red.

'The sand.' I lean forward, looking at my fungus. 'I've been working on it for weeks. Weeks. It could have been important. It could have been . . . penicillin.'

'Bad luck.' He shrugs. 'But it wasn't me.'

He's lying. I jerk forward, bang the jar on the floor, then charge. Leo yelps, but I grab him by his legs and he comes crashing down onto the rug. He tries to hit back, but I have his arms pinned behind his head. I lean over him so that all he can see is my face. 'You little creep. Why did you do it?' I press hard on his weedy arms. 'Tell me or I'll break your thumb.'

Leo is scared. I can see it in his eyes. I put pressure on his left-hand thumb. More pressure, more. 'Okay, I'll tell . . . but . . . let me go.'

'Tell first.' I press harder. The thumb crunches. 'Now.'

'You weren't supposed to bring the fungus,' he stutters. 'Anna told me.'

'So what?' I twist his arm.

'Ugh. Everyone thinks you're so great. Well, you're not. What about the orange rock? It's graffiti. I should tell.'

'As if it was graffiti.' As if Mum and Rob would care.

'You're so dumb you even wrote SuperJack backwards. I'll tell them.' Leo is shaking. 'I'll tell.' Leo shakes his head.

'Well, do it. See if I care.' I put more pressure on his arm.

'Stop, Jack. Stop, stop. You're hurting me.'

'You destroyed my fungus. Why would you do that? Why?'

'I don't know.'

'Sure you do.' I twist his arm a bit more.

'Stop, Jack. It's about stuff. Stuff like thermometers and the orange juice squisher.'

What is Leo talking about? I still hold on to his arm. 'What is wrong with you?'

'You do stuff with Dad like making shelves in the garage. He told me that.' Leo's voice catches into a gulp. 'Dad thinks you're smart, Jack. You make things.' He looks at me. 'Like fungus.' He whispers, 'You even saved Nanna.'

I stare at him. 'Do you want her dead?'

'No, Jack,' Leo pleads. 'it's just that Dad is always talking about you. All the time.'

'Me?' I start to let go of Leo's arms. I don't get it. Leo is Rob's favourite. 'You're his son, not me.'

'Am I?' Leo blinks hard. 'He hardly visits me. He doesn't know me and I don't know him. That's how it feels.' He swallows a sob. 'And when he eventually comes to see me, he brings all of you. Why did he do that? I'm not that important, that's why.'

'It's because you're important that Rob brought us. To make us all a family. Can't you see that?' I let Leo go, and lean back against the wall next to my fungus. Leo slowly gets up, then sags onto the bottom bunk. I watch him for a while. He watches me. 'Were you going to light a fire today?'

He shakes his head. 'As if I would. You'd have to be scum to light a bushfire. Is that what you think I am?'

I stare at him, unsure. 'So why do you carry the lighter, then?'

Leo stammers. 'Because it's Dad's. It's my dad's. It belonged to his father in the war. Dad doesn't know I took it.' He speaks so quietly I can hardly hear him. 'I've had it ever since he left. It's got his initials on it.'

My head is throbbing. I don't want to feel sad for Leo. I look down at my feet, trying to catch my breath.

He kicks the legs of the bunk. 'I didn't win the kangaroo. I was burying the wrapping, that's all,' he mutters. 'I wanted to impress Anna.'

There is no talking. I don't know what to feel. Leo

destroyed my fungus. Leo misses his father. I think about that for a while. We just sit thinking. I've never asked Leo about himself, really. I don't know why I never did that. I ask now. 'So what's it like living in Port?'

He looks at his hands. 'Good, but . . .' He stops.

I wait. Leo doesn't say anything for five minutes, while I stare at my failed fungus. Then he speaks. 'Even though Dad sends money, Mum has never got any.' He stutters. 'Mum's boyfriend is a real user.' I know about having no money. Leo whispers, stammering out the words. 'It's not the same as with you and Dad.'

Rob. No, it's not the same.

Leo takes a deep breath. 'Please don't tell Dad, or anyone, about the fungus.'

I mumble, 'Okay.'

'It was a low thing to do.'

I look him in the eyes. They are watery. I shake my head. There will be other experiments. 'No more garbage, Leo. Okay?' I turn off the light, climb onto the top bunk. 'Okay, Leo?'

'Okay, Jack.'

I close my eyes but can't sleep. Thoughts and pictures go through my mind. I smile at Mum and her star jumps and Rob's great orange juice. Samantha is laughing at my jokes. Nanna choking. I cough, remembering the taste of vomit. But it is a great thing to have made Nanna breathe again. And there is Anna. I'll grow more fungus . . . Suddenly a buzz zips through my head and it doesn't hurt.

Morning. I creep out of the bedroom, because Leo is still asleep. I am carrying my fungus jar. I chuck it out.

There is a note that Mum and Rob have left to go to the hospital. *Gone to collect Nanna.*

I check on the girls. Still sleeping. I want them to get up so I stomp around the bedroom. No reaction. I slump onto the rug in the middle of the floor. Movement at last. Anna rolls onto her side. Girls awake. About time. 'Thought you two were practising to be Sleeping Beauty One and Sleeping Beauty Two.'

Samantha yawns as she stumbles out of her bed. 'Well, you're not the Prince who woke her up.'

'More like a frog.' Anna pretends to be a frog and croaks. 'You'll have to get out of our room. We're getting dressed.'

That could be hours. I slouch onto the lounge, looking out of the window and watching for Mum and Rob to come back. I turn on the TV. Cartoons.

Suddenly there is a horn beeping. It's them. I race outside.

'Hold on, hold on.' Rob opens the door for Nanna.

'Nanna are you all right?' Her face is pale, her wrinkles are creased together, her hair is sticking out in hard bits around her bandage and her wrist is still in plaster.

Mum helps Nanna wobble inside and settles her into her lounge chair. The girls arrive with Leo behind them. Nanna beams. 'So good to see you children.'

Mum brings Nanna a cup of tea and two crackers. I try to think of a joke. A joke will make her feel she's back on track. 'Hey Nanna, listen to this.' She looks up at me with cracker bits stuck to the sides of her mouth.

'Old Nanna Hubbard
Went to the cupboard
To get her mad doggy a crumb.
When she got there
The cupboard was bare
So the dog took a bite from her bum.'

Everyone laughs. 'Poor dog.' Samantha hits my arm. 'And Nanna's bum probably tasted better than the crumb.'

Nanna chuckles. I am on a roll now. Joke King, they call me.

'There once was a roly-poly Nanna
Who fell on her wrist and broke it.
It would have been wise
If she'd opened her eyes
But she didn't, and flattened her cookies instead.'

Nanna is smiling when Mum brings her a glass of water and the hospital pain relief tablets. She takes them. 'I need to have a rest now.' Mum and I help Nanna up from her chair. As she shuffles towards her bedroom, she turns a little towards us and sniffs. 'I'm so lucky to have you all.'

'We're lucky to have you, Nanna.' Samantha is too quick. I wanted to say that.

Mum shuts Nanna's door, looks at us and blows out a whoosh of air. 'Lunch.' Mum is humming. Everything must be all right. I bet she'll do a star jump soon. I take out the bread for sandwiches. Leo helps me and that's okay. Anna is setting the table and Rob has his orange juice squisher ready for action. Samantha is standing next to him, of course.

Everything is getting back to normal. Samantha is munching a tomato sandwich, the sun is shining, the waves are rolling onto the sand.

Rob reads my mind. 'Beach, everyone?'

There are yahoos. Last sandwiches stuffed into mouths. Mum isn't coming because she wants to stay with Nanna. 'I have to do the last load of washing anyway.' She crinkles her eyes at us. No one dares says a word.

Rob jumps up from the table, then disappears into his room. Suddenly he reappears and everyone bursts out laughing. He is standing in the middle of the room with his skinny legs, shrunken T-shirt and skin-tight shorts. 'Nothing wrong with them.' He winks at me. 'Your mother is artistic and my shorts are earth-coloured.' He dumps four multicoloured beach towels in a pile. Mum goes red. Rob tickles her, and swirls her around until she is laughing. Mum will never, ever live it down.

We all grab a towel and head off to the beach. Yellow sand and blue surf. The flags are flapping, marking where it is safe to swim. Two lifesavers are on patrol. 'Race you.' I am panting as I hit the water. It's warm. Rob is in just after me. We catch some great waves. Rob really knows how to body surf. Leo does too. Rob taught Leo to body surf when he was little. I feel all right about that somehow. Rob runs into the swell just at the right time and rides the best waves. He gives me a few tips. I have been catching the wave too early. We ride some fast ones right into shore. I spy on Samantha, and when she's not looking I dive for her. She splashes me. Anna joins her, but I don't play for long. I swim after Rob. The surf is big.

I am waiting for the right moment to catch a wave when I see it. I gulp a mouthful of salt water. Splutter, cough. I see it again. Grey fin. My heart is a beating drum. Panic. Sharks. They have been known to take a man with just one attack. I'm totally rigid in the water, bobbing up and down with the waves like a petrified twig. Don't move. Don't move. Maybe it won't notice me. Quiet. Mum won't know what has happened if I'm eaten.

Mum needs me. Oh no, it's coming my way. I am dead. Dead. Splashing. It is going for me, for sure. I'm going to make a dash for it. Breathe, breathe. Swim fast. Rob grabs me. Thank God. Rob, Rob. The thumping drum is slowing down. He is pointing to the fins. There is more than one now. Then there are flippers. Black fan tails. Diving tails and fins, jumping through the waves, somersaulting with laughing faces.

Dolphins, dolphins!

Gasp, pant, wheeze. I am slowly breathing again. Rob rubs my wet hair. 'Don't worry. I've taken them for sharks myself.'

The girls and Leo are paddling towards us. We all watch for a while as the dolphins glide and leap through the water. Better surfers than we will ever be. We slowly move towards them, watching them tumble until we are there swimming with them.

It is one of those great moments in life.

Scrabble

Dolphins, dolphins are all that we can talk about as we walk back. Rob stops to buy a newspaper and a carton of milk at the corner shop. Samantha tells the shopkeeper that she swam with dolphins. 'Lucky you!' The shopkeeper smiles. I can see he wishes he was as lucky.

As soon as we open the door to the apartment Samantha charges into her room to find her dolphin necklace. 'I'm going to wear it forever.'

We bombard Mum and Nanna with everything that happened. 'Dolphins are amazing.' Anna's eyes light up.

'Jack thought they were sharks at first.' Samantha runs back wearing her necklace.

There are a few Jack jokes about sharks and dolphins. But I don't care, because I swam with dolphins. I plunk myself next to Rob, who winks at me. I wink back. Mum heads for the kitchen, dancing around. She swishes her arms from left to right. Star jumps. Suddenly there is a crash. Mum has star jumped into the garbage bin. Her hair is perpendicular and her elbows covered in sticky orange. Everyone is laughing, but not me. This is a great photo moment. I snatch my camera. She is struggling out of the bin with an orange peel stuck to her bum. Snap. 'Don't take that, Jack. Pleassse.' Snap. Snap.

'Sorry.' A photographer has to be tough.

'You've taken some great pictures, Jack.' Rob looks at Leo. 'Do you have a camera, Leo?'

'No, Dad.' Leo glances at me.

'Well, maybe I can fix that up.'

I feel fine when Rob says that. I have a camera already anyway.

'Chocolate cake.' Mum is carrying the biggest, gooiest mud cake into the lounge room. 'I baked it while you were at the beach.' She is flushed. Mum thinks she is the best cook in the world. She puts it onto the coffee table. 'Who wants a piece?' Samantha sticks her finger in the chocolate frosting.

'That's disgusting. Don't.' I knock her hand away.

Mum starts slicing the cake. She gives a big piece to Nanna, whose face lights up. Mum bats her eyelashes at Rob. I laugh at her. 'It's been a special holiday, hasn't it?' she says.

'Yes Mum.' I roll my eyes. I hope Mum doesn't go into one of her gooey moments.

'Except for Nanna's accident. But Jack was a hero, so that was special too.'

I can't take it, even for chocolate cake. Mum, STOP. World peace is better than this.

Anna and Samantha are nodding.

'I love you all, and . . .' She waits. 'Rob . . .' Then she waits some more.

What is this about? I kick Samantha under the table. 'Don't do that, Jack.' Samantha kicks me back.

Mum lifts her left hand. On her fourth finger is a gold ring. I look at Rob's left hand. He slips a gold ring on his fourth finger.

What? Mum and Rob are standing next to each other now. What does this mean? I scratch my arm. Samantha is already in cuddle mode. She is squashing Rob so hard that his eyes look like they'll pop out. Anna is holding Nanna's hand. Leo and I stare at each other. What is Leo thinking?

'We'd like to make it official when we get home. Maybe we can have a small ceremony in the park with a celebrant.' Mum looks at Samantha. 'Would you be my flower girl?' Samantha is beaming. Mum turns to Anna. 'Would you like to be a flower girl too?'

Anna and Samantha are so excited they hug each other, then Mum. Oh no, it's mass hug time. I have to leave. I have to think.

'Jack. What do you say?' Mum escapes from Samantha's octopus grip.

'Don't ask me to be a page boy.'

She laughs. 'I wouldn't do that to you.'

My head is swirling.

Rob reaches for Leo's arm. 'Would you be . . .' Rob stops, 'my best man?'

I can't swallow. I know Rob has to ask Leo. Leo is his son, not like me.

Leo nods. 'That'd be good, Dad.' I wonder if he really thinks that.

Rob looks at me. 'Will you be my other best man, Jack?'

My chest expands like a huge bubble of gum. 'Yes.'

Samantha is babbling about flower girl dresses and daisies in her hair. When Anna joins in, I escape into the bathroom. I take the longest shower ever. Sand is stuck between my legs and in my ears. I wash, then scrub my hair with Rob's shampoo. The water beating down on me feels good. Rob will be my dad. 'My dad.' I repeat 'dad', trying to fit it inside my head. It sounds good, I think.

Leo is waiting at the bathroom door to go in. He is still sandy too. 'I've used up all the hot water.' Leo's faces crunches into a whinge. 'Just joking.'

I look into the girls' bedroom. The CD is playing Samantha music. Anna has the SCRABBLE board laid out. Floppy is lying next to Samantha, of course. 'Are you going to play, Jack?'

I get my pillow from my room and crash next to Samantha. Anna starts with the first word. 'QUICK.'

'Good word,' I say. 'Lots of points.'

'KAYAK.' Samantha is smart at this game, even though she is younger. I like the word KAYAK because it can be spelt backwards or forwards. It's a winner word.

We have the board half full of words when I put down 'GOLF'. It must be in my brain because of Rob. Then this unexpected question pops into my mind. 'Do you ever think about our real dad, Samantha?'

'No. Rob is our real dad.'

'Step-dad.' A throb zips through the back of my head. I rub my neck.

'Rob is really your dad, Jack.' Anna's chocolate drop eyes sparkle. 'He's the one who's here for you.'

I nod. 'But Leo isn't my brother. He's not.'

'He'll be your step-brother. You'll have to see what happens, but he's part of your family now.'

'And Anna and I are going to be flower girls.'

'Very interesting.' I groan.

There is a knock on the door. It opens and we see a bit of daisy skirt. 'Can I come in?' Mum has red hibiscuses in her hands. She gives one to Anna and one to Samantha and they put them behind their ears. 'You girls are beautiful.' She is right about that. Mum sits cross-legged next to me on the floor. She says nothing for ages. She just watches us playing. Suddenly, she coughs so loudly we stop. Samantha rubs Mum's back, but it is not that type of cough. Mum presses her lip, fiddles with her flower, curls her skirt, until we all laugh.

'Do you want to say something, Mum?'

She nods. 'Yes.' Big breath. 'Are you okay about the gold rings?' She pauses. 'About Rob?'

Samantha squeezes Floppy. 'I love Rob even when he's dumb and teases me.'

'Jack? This won't work without you.'

'It's okay.' As I say it, it feels like the truth. I think I mean it. I think I do.

Mum's voice is soft. 'We have to all work at it. Sometimes we'll get angry at each other and sometimes we'll laugh. We've got to forgive each other, be kind.'

I give a nervous laugh. '"No terrorists." Sorry, I couldn't help that, Mum.'

Mum half-smiles at my joke. 'It's a bigger family, with more things to fight about, more things to sort out.' Mum takes my hand. 'Jack, you've been amazing. I know how hard it is to suddenly share a room, suddenly have a father, suddenly have Leo. I know, Jack.'

I nod. We talk for ages and everything feels

better. Then Leo arrives and we get back to the game. I glance at him. Maybe one day Mum will talk to him too.

Mum and Samantha play together. They win as usual. Anna comes second, I come third and Leo last. 'Don't worry, Leo. We play a lot of SCRABBLE. You'll just have to play with us lots more.' Mum smiles at him. He smiles back at her for the first time on this holiday.

We are packing up the SCRABBLE when Rob announces that we're spending the last afternoon of our holiday at Surfers Paradise. 'Do you want to go?'

He doesn't have to ask twice. 'Can we see the Believe It or Not! Museum? Please, Rob? Pleassse?'

'We'll see.'

Surfers Paradise. Rob parks in a car park that's close to everything, since Nanna can't walk too far — if you call it walking. She is slower than ever. We all have to blubber along like land-locked seals. At last we stop at a café near the beach. The beach looks excellent. It is bursting with sunbakers and sandcastle builders. As we sit down at a table, street musicians wander past strumming guitars. A man sets up near our table and does a jig with a sulphur-crested white cockatoo on his shoulder. Then Rob does something generous, really generous. He pulls out four $20 notes. 'That's the entry fee for the museum and anything else you like.'

That is even better than Mum's bribery. 'Thank you, thank you, thank you.' We all bombard Rob until he pushes us away.

I really want to see the tallest man in the world. We don't hang around the café for long. Mum and Rob want to talk to Nanna. So, we are off. Samantha spots it first. Water is gushing out of a tap and it's connected to nothing. 'There,' she squeals.

The museum is excellent. There are amazing galleries of human bones, skulls, the Lord's Prayer engraved on a grain of rice, a shrunken head. It is all horrible or weird. Then we see him dressed in a three-piece grey suit, wearing glasses. He is 8' 11" — nearly three metres tall — and made of wax. I read out aloud, '*The tallest man of all time. Robert Wadlow in 1940 weighed 440 pounds.* That's about 200 kilos. That's what I call heavy.' I take a photo of everyone next to Robert. 'You're all shrimps. Ha, ha.'

Samantha has to close her eyes when she sees the Lighthouse Man of China who walked the streets with a candle inserted in a hole in his skull. Anna puts her arm around her. She is kind like that. Leo finds the Human Stunts and Feats Theatre. It is screening some idiot who goes over the massive Niagara Falls in a barrel. Wild water crashes like massive demolition explosives. The waterfalls are huge and the barrel is small. It's dark, and I squeeze Anna's hand as we both watch in amazement. She squeezes back.

Anna wants to shop. 'I'd like to buy something for Papa and Mamma.' She gets twin red flower Hawaiian shirts. They will really look good wearing them in summer in the fruitologist market. The shirts will match the mangoes and peaches. Leo buys a T-shirt for his mother. He doesn't buy one for her boyfriend. I have to get Christopher a present, since he's minding Hector. I notice a snake box. The snake's head sizzles out when you open it. I buy the snake box. Then I see it. Oh no, I've got no money left. It is the last one, and cheap. Half-price just because one eye is missing. I don't care about a missing eye. It is about fifteen centimetres long. I count the webbed toes. Yes, five on each foot. Four unwebbed ones on each hand. Looks all good. Anna turns her nose up in disgust. Well, she isn't a scientist, so she wouldn't understand.

I seriously beg Samantha for her money. 'Yes, I'll do the washing up every night for two weeks.' 'No, I won't make any more dog jokes' (at least for a while). 'Yes, I'll be your slave.'

Samantha laughs. 'As if.' I'm getting desperate, but she understands that I am a scientist and need it. She hands over money, but it's not enough. Then Leo does something incredible. He digs in his pocket. 'Here, take this. That'll be enough.'

I buy it. An original one-eyed cane toad.

Mum waves when she sees us coming back. Everyone is amazed at my cane toad. He is a star.

Not even the Hawaiian shirts can outshine Wally. That's what I'm calling him. Wish he was alive. Since he's not, his spirit and stuffed body will at least have a great home with me. Mum says Wally can't sit at the table while we have our milkshakes. I put him on my lap. Don't want anyone to step on him.

Since Nanna can't walk, Rob does a twilight tourist drive along the beach front, then around the rivers and lakes. Samantha and Anna point out every frangipani tree. Nanna and Mum love the tropical gardens with the birds of paradise and palms. I love Wally.

Tonight is our last night on holidays. After dinner we pack up everything except for toothbrushes. I can't believe it has already been a week. Tomorrow we're dropping off Leo at Port, then it's Sydney non-stop. I smile. Except for Rob's two-hourly 'Stop, Revive, Survive' break. He is a maniac about that. There won't be a Big Banana stop on the way back. I just know it.

Mum puts her arm through Rob's. 'Let's go for a last walk. Anyone want to join us?'

Anna and I are ready. Samantha and Nanna are too busy playing cards. Leo is plugged into his computer game. Some things don't change.

We stroll along the pathway bordering the sand. Mum and Rob are talking seriously. I hear the word 'Nanna' whispered a few times.

'Hey, can we go down to the beach?'

'Yes,' Mum and Rob say together.

We take off our shoes, then wander down to the edge of the water. Even though it is night, the sea is still warm. 'That was nice of Leo to give you his money to buy the cane toad.'

'You mean Wally?' I smile. Leo is all right. He will never be my best friend like Christopher, but he's all right.

We run towards the sea as the tide draws the water backwards. Then we run back as waves crash on the shore. Anna trips and the waves spray her shorts, but she doesn't mind. She laughs as we flick sand from side to side with our toes. We march around a complicated sandcastle with one square tower that's been half washed away. 'There's the moat and a drawbridge.' Anna bends to look at the silvery mother-of-pearl shell pressed into the tower. The lights of Surfers Paradise are in the distance. 'They look like stars.' Anna runs her fingers through her licorice curls. A tingle travels through me. We wander along the beach for a while. We laugh about Nanna's purple underpants, joke about the goanna attack, talk about swimming with the dolphins. I take Anna's hand. It's soft. Then I kiss her cheek. Red flushes spread over my face. Luckily Anna can't see me. We walk a bit further, then stop to look out to sea.

Chapter 16

Going Home

New day. Crack of dawn. Is it morning? The sun isn't up yet. Oh, what a night. Great dreams. The beach. Anna. I close my eyes again. Who is shaking me? 'Stop,' I turn onto my stomach. More shaking. I blearily open my eyes. 'Mum?' Oh yes, we're leaving. 'Too early.'

'Come on, Jack.' Mum's fuzzy blonde hair tickles the tip of my nose.

'Yeah, yeah.' Moan. I clump down the bunk ladder. Everyone is up. I don't know how it happened but it is five-thirty in the morning and we are all ready to go.

Rob hangs his thermometer at the back of the car. 'Checking the temperature.' Rob advises us that the temperature was perfect on the Gold Coast.

'Between thirty-two and thirty-six degrees every day.' There are a few thermometer jokes about how Rob is hot except for his brain, which is still defrosting. Rob ignores them.

We clamber into the car. I am sitting next to Anna and holding Wally. Samantha is hugging Floppy. Nanna is belted in the back seat next to Leo. I want to say a joke, but it's dark and I'm half-asleep and my mind isn't into gear yet. I keep thinking about Rob's weather report. The ignition clicks and the engine starts. Mum's music quietly hums and zzzzzz . . . We are all sleeping.

'Breakfast,' Mum's voice tinkles. I open my eyes, yawn, blink. There is daylight and I'm hungry. We are all hungry. Hmmm. Breakfast. I have the works. Two fried eggs, bacon, tomato and sausages with toast.

'Jack, you'd better eat that up super fast.' Rob flashes a look at Anna.

'Jack has a super appetite.' Anna hides her dimples behind a smile.

What is everyone going on about?

'Except he likes to eat "super" backwards.' Mum twirls a curl. 'Super duper Jack.'

Oh right. I get it, someone has blabbed. 'Was it you, Leo?'

He laughs. 'No way.'

'So who told? Who told?'

Samantha sticks Floppy in my face. 'None of your business.'

'We might just have a look at that SuperJack boulder when we drop Leo home.' Rob makes a right handed fist.

'Great.' I groan.

'Jack, limerick,' Mum calls out as we get back into the car. 'A super one, darling.'

I groan again. 'Okay, limericks.' Samantha is yapping away. (Dog joke.) 'Keep quiet. We're doing the one where everyone says a line.'

'Don't know what you mean.' Samantha is unhelpful.

Rob is already zooming along the highway. There are a few SuperJacks yelled out. I shout, 'Topic is Nanna.' Nanna beams of course. She loves being the topic. Everyone shuts up because no one wants to hurt Nanna's feelings. I start.

'There was an old Nanna from Surfers (me)
Who loved swimming like a porpoise' (I wanted to say dolphins, but it doesn't rhyme)
'She slid down the path' (Leo adds)
'And fractured her arm' (Rob)
'So Nanna swam crooked instead.' (Samantha)

Samantha's line doesn't quite rhyme, but it's a good start. I nudge Leo. 'You choose the topic for the next limerick.'

'Pig.'

Phew. Glad it wasn't SuperJack.

'That's terrific, Leo.' Mum cups her hands next to

her head pretending they are pig's ears. She thinks she is funny. She is NOT.

'Meet Miss Piggy Piggle' (Mum)
'Watch her give a wiggle' (Nanna)
'Her husband is Rob' (Samantha)
'What a dumb knob' (Me, ha, ha)
'And both of them make you giggle.' (Anna — that's so cute)

We are all laughing when Mum asks right out of nowhere, 'Do you think you'd like to live in a house?' She turns around to look at us.

'House. Is that the next limerick, Mum?' Samantha squeals.

'No.' Mum reaches her hand across to her. 'Would you like to live in a house, with a garden?'

'A garden,' Samantha repeats.

'A house,' I echo. We are all a bit staggered. What does Mum mean? 'We live in a unit.'

'Yes, but Rob and I want to buy a house.' Mum takes a breath. 'There will be a room for Nanna.' Mum looks at Leo. 'And Leo when he visits. Leo, you can sleep in your own room, too.'

Nanna nods and her teeth wobble forward a bit. She obviously knows all about this. Her green eyes have tears in them.

Samantha has been quiet, which is very un-Samantha-like. Suddenly she bursts out, 'A garden?

Oh a garden, Mum. There'll be room for a puppy. A real puppy. Can I have a puppy?'

I tickle Floppy. 'But he'll be jealous.'

Samantha hugs Floppy really hard. 'Please Mum. Please Rob.'

Mum and Rob smile at each other. 'Yes.'

Samantha is speechless for the first time in her life. She just keeps hugging Floppy.

This is all too amazing. I need time to think. I stare out of the window watching the gum trees swoosh by. A house, Rob and Mum, Nanna living with us.

'We'll find a house not too far away from where we live now.' Mum smiles. 'Not far from the best fruitologist in Sydney.'

Anna's laugh sings through the car.

I stammer, 'Rob, do you think we can have our own workshop?'

'We'll have one, Jack. For sure,' he calls out. 'And Leo can use it too.'

I shake my head. Leo won't use it. It'll be Rob's and mine. But Leo can have his own things there. It's fair. There has to be a Leo computer bench for sure. I stare at Rob's golf ball head and Mum's blonde fuzz. Imagine the wedding. They are going to look so funny. I start to laugh.

Suddenly Nanna sees a big fishing poster.

Fish.

Nanna's eyes light up. Oh no. She turns to Leo. 'Do you know when Jack was a baby, he swallowed a . . .'

I AM JACK
Susanne Gervay

Jack likes going to school. He enjoys learning.
   George Hamel calls Jack — Bum Head.
   All the kids at school call Jack — Bum Head.
   Jack's in BIG trouble . . . school is getting dangerous.
   Nobody seems to want to listen. Until one day . . .

'*I Am Jack* celebrates kids. Unique, valuable kids. Bullying isolates and victimises children. I Am Jack shows them that they are not alone and can win against bullying.'

LIFE EDUCATION AUSTRALIA

ISBN 978 0 207 19905 9